I0551576

In Eden's Shadow

A. L. Swanson

Copyright ©2013 A. L. Swanson
Goldenlight Publishing™
goldenlightpublishing.com

Cover Art by Manthos Lappas
http://mlappas.deviantart.com

ISBN-13: 978-0615936581 (Custom)
ISBN-10: 061593658X

Acknowledgements

I'd like to thank my friends Lucas and Phil. Thank you for all of your help throughout the publishing process. I couldn't have done it without you.

I'd like to thank my family. You've always been there for me and supported me. Thanks Mom, Chad, Robin, Keri, Haley and Hanna. And to my dad, who I know is watching over me and helping to guide me on my path through life. I love you all.

I wish to thank all of the friends that have helped me through the years. I appreciate everything you've done for me along the way, and for reading and critiquing my work. Thanks Mike, Pete, Deb, Sara, Mary, Doug, Nick, Boyde, Coby, Sarah, Tim, Melanie and Jimmy.

Thanks to some of the most influential teachers in my life Rosemary, Hersh and Bill.

Lastly, I'd like to thank Manthos. The artwork you provided for the book is phenomenal.

PROLOGUE

Michael tore his sword from his enemy's chest and stepped clear of the falling body. The landscape of Heaven was splattered with the blood of angels. Friends and brothers had been split into enemies and allies by blasphemous promises and jealous tempers, and bodies were spread across the trampled grass to the far horizon. Around Michael, many angels still battled, while others dropped their blades to mourn the fallen.

Michael peeled the long, bloody dark hair from his forehead and brushed it back over the top of his head. He lifted his sword with weary arms and moved toward the angels who still fought. He stepped over bodies as he walked, unable to distinguish friend from foe. Suddenly, he stopped, feeling Lucifer's approach before seeing him.

Michael turned to watch the traitor cross the battlefield. Several angels attempted to intercept him but were easily cut down. Lucifer walked up to Michael and stopped.

The two angels watched each other, unmoving, statuesque. Lucifer's short blond hair stirred in the breeze; his features were soft, but there was madness in his eyes. Michael's features were chiseled and his eyes steeled in determination.

"Have you realized the folly of not joining us?" Lucifer asked.

"The only folly was you turning against God and your brothers," Michael said. "How could you do this? You were the greatest among us. You were what we all strived to become."

"I did this for us," Lucifer said. "I love you all as brothers, but we have bowed to the humans for too long. We are their superiors, yet we are ordered by our father to demean ourselves by serving them. I am offering freedom from this life of servitude. Under the reign of God, we were little more than slaves to the will of those lesser creatures. Under my reign, we will be slaves to no one. We will rebuild our family and create a new Heaven where no one will be forced to serve."

"We would serve no one but you. Under your reign, we would be slaves to your will and whim. We were created by God, and it is our duty to help the humans by guiding them to our father's word."

"Father only cares about what we can do for him. He cares more for those humans than he does for us. Can you not feel it?"

"That's not true," Michael said. "He cares for all of us, while you only care for yourself. You want to overthrow God only to fulfill your own dreams of power."

"Silence!" Lucifer snapped. "It's obvious that you can't be reasoned with. Your blind devotion to God is what will lead to your destruction. I'm sorry, but since you stand in my way, I have no choice but to destroy you."

"I'm sorry as well, but it's obvious that your madness has consumed you. Farewell, brother."

Lucifer leapt at Michael, swinging his sword in a wide arc. Michael brought his sword up, barely catching the blow.

Sparks flew as the two weapons connected, seemingly screaming in protest. Lucifer pushed forward, attacking fanatically, while Michael fell back, trying desperately to parry.

Michael stopped his retreat and forced himself to hold his ground. His breathing was heavy, and sweat ran into his eyes. He tried driving Lucifer back, but couldn't penetrate his defenses. Their blades clashed and the metal smoked. Michael tried to block a quick sideswipe, but his reflexes were a moment too slow, and Lucifer's sword bit deep into his left side.

Michael stumbled, clutching his side. Blood ran through the white chain armor and between his fingers. Lucifer charged at Michael, leaving himself open. He had no patience; it would be his downfall.

Michael fell backward and Lucifer's sword whistled over him. Michael brought his sword up, drove it into Lucifer's abdomen, and let go. The momentum of the charging angel carried him over the top of Michael, and Lucifer landed hard on his back. Michael stood and approached Lucifer, pulling his sword free. Lucifer rolled over and started to push himself up, but Michael stepped on the fallen angel's back, forcing him to the ground. He lifted his sword to strike down the writhing creature beneath him but hesitated. Instead, he grabbed Lucifer by the hair and pulled him along behind him.

Lucifer struggled, but couldn't break Michael's grip. Michael dragged him to the sharp cliff at the edge of the battlefield and threw him to the ground. Lucifer stood and looked over the edge at the seemingly endless drop before turning back to Michael.

"What now?" Lucifer asked. "Will you kill me for your God?"

"No," Michael said, "I will cast you out."

Michael grabbed Lucifer and shoved him over the edge. Lucifer clawed at the air and managed to grab the ring of keys on Michael's belt. Michael lurched forward as the weight threatened to pull him over the edge as well. Michael braced himself, drew his sword, and brought the blade down on the gold key ring, shattering it. Michael watched as Lucifer fell screaming toward Earth. Then he noticed a black key spiraling after him. All he could do was watch helplessly as the key of the Abyss tumbled away. He debated going after it, but he was Heaven's General now, and the battle wasn't over yet. He turned back to the fighting, leaving the key to land where it may. God would be upset, but there was little he could have done. Eventually, to keep it out of Lucifer's hands, someone would have to retrieve it. For now, though, there was little to do but finish the battle.

CHAPTER 1 - HEAVEN

Raiel sat across from Dokiel, calmly polishing the blade of his sword. He sat cross-legged in the warm grass as the sun warmed his back. The droning words of the elder angel were reaching his ears but wouldn't be retained beyond the next pass of his polishing cloth. He already knew the mission, and all the constant talking was nothing more than an irritation. Just because it was his first trip to Earth didn't mean that he would suddenly lose his senses. On the contrary, the other angels believed that his unbiased mind would be much better at sensing the key of the Abyss than would any of the more battle-ravaged archangels. Nearly all the archangels had been to Earth several times and experienced the various pleasures that could only be found there. While they still managed to remain true to God, they had become tainted.

Raiel glanced up at Dokiel a moment before returning his attention to his work. Dokiel was soft and knew nothing of battle. His pale skin was unblemished by scars and wrapped in silken robes. Other than his short dark hair and brown eyes, there was no color to him. Raiel's own body was athletic and marked with scars from many battles. His eyes were blue and his blond hair was the same length as Dokiel's. He wore a pair of loose white pants and a matching shirt. They gave him more freedom of movement in battle and signified him as a warrior. The two angels were complete opposites in every way, but Dokiel still thought he knew how Raiel should best complete his mission.

Raiel stared at his reflection in the mirror shine of his sword a moment before sheathing it. He had tried to sit patiently through the constant warnings and advice of the other angels, but his patience had reached its limit.

There was concern that his lack of experience would put him in danger and allow the enemy a sizable advantage. In a world filled with so much evil and temptation, a young mind could easily be twisted. It was a recurring theme in his talks with the elder angels—one that he felt had been adequately driven into his head.

Raiel looked up, aware that his mind had been wandering. Dokiel had stopped talking and was watching him. The elder angel's frustration with his young pupil was apparent, which only added to Raiel's own.

"How do you ever expect to succeed if you don't know what you're supposed to be doing?" Dokiel asked.

"I already know what I'm supposed to be doing and this constant nagging isn't helping."

"You don't seem to realize how difficult this mission will be. If you don't know what to expect, you're liable to be sidetracked. There are many things on Earth to tempt an innocent such as you."

"I'm not as innocent as everyone seems to think. I wouldn't have gotten to where I am today if I were."

"We are all aware of your hard work and sacrifices in the name of God, but we also know what you'll be facing on Earth. Even the strongest of angels can be swayed by temptation, and we cannot afford for anything to go wrong."

"Nothing will go wrong. I have been fully informed of everything I will encounter."

"You may know, but there's a big difference between knowing and feeling. You may know everything that will be required of you on Earth, but once you are there and you start to experience all the new feelings and emotions, all the knowledge in existence may not be enough to save you. You need to know how to handle those feelings and use them to help you on your quest."

"You worry too much. I will go to Earth, track down the key, and return with it. If I run into any of the fallen ones, I will destroy them and continue with my quest."

"I wish I felt as confident about your mission as you do. I think you're getting into much more than you can imagine."

"I appreciate your concern, but everything will work out."

"I truly hope so," Dokiel said. "Either way, it will soon be out of our hands and into yours. Then there will be nothing for us to do but witness your success or your failure. Now, I know it may be pointless to ask, but do you have any questions before you depart?"

"No, sir, none at all. You have thoroughly prepared me for anything I might encounter on Earth, and I truly believe that I am ready."

"In that case, I will wish you luck and leave you to enjoy the remainder of your time here. I hope you will use this time to meditate on the task at hand and continue your preparations."

"Thank you, Dokiel. I'll do that."

Dokiel smiled at the young angel before turning to take his leave. He loved Raiel and knew the strength he possessed, but a dark feeling was weaving through his thoughts. He tried pushing it from his mind, but it lingered. So much was riding on Raiel. If he should fail, it would allow Satan's forces to release all the plagues of the Bible upon Earth. The death and destruction would be unimaginable.

The decision to send Raiel wasn't easily reached. Many of the elder angels had expressed concerns about his youth and inexperience; but in the end, he was the only chance they had. Dokiel prayed he would succeed. If he didn't, then everyone on Earth would suffer for his failure.

CHAPTER 2 - HELL

Jetrel walked through the dark maze of tunnels with the ease of experience. He knew every inch of every tunnel throughout this maze of fire and smoke. How many millions of years had he spent here in Hell, wandering these tunnels? He hadn't bothered to keep count. Even if he had, he doubted it would have been an accurate one. Time moved differently here, and the days seemed to blur into one another. He had heard that one day on Earth was equal to 100 days in Hell, but he believed it to be a lot more than that.

Jetrel brushed his long, dark hair out of his face as he walked along, absently using his sword to poke at the victims of eternal torment he encountered. They screamed as the blade split their skin and organs, but Jetrel barely noticed. His mind was on the mission for which he had been chosen.

This was to be his first trip to Earth, and he was concentrating on what needed to be done. It was his first mission and he wanted it to go well. If he impressed the master, maybe he could do something more than simply supervise the torment of souls. It was a lot better than being one of the victims, but after so many years of the same routine, it had lost its appeal.

He had been told that Earth was full of sin and that a demon could easily become distracted and lose sight of the objective. He was determined not to do that. He would succeed no matter what. If the master was impressed, perhaps he would be allowed to return to Earth and have a little fun later.

Jetrel sat down on a bench crudely carved out of a large piece of red stone. He looked out across the sea of flames and screaming souls in front of him. He knew his mission well, and he knew that Heaven would be sending an angel to find the key. Facing an angel in battle didn't worry him. Killing an angel was something he had been looking forward to for centuries. He worried about what would happen if the angel found the key first and returned it to Heaven. No one knew where the key was, and for all he knew, the angel could end up arriving on Earth nearly on top of it.

Jetrel stared at the lake of fire in front of him as the flames jumped into the darkness above, illuminating the scorched stone ceiling. He was apathetic to the sights and smells he experienced as part of his everyday life. He never took the time to look at the faces of the people he was tormenting; he never thought of them as anything more than scenery. Now he watched the twisted, screaming faces amidst the flames and imagined being one of them—spending eternity drowning in fire, clawing at the souls around you to try to push yourself above it for a moment of respite, and screaming and praying to a God who could no longer hear you or no longer cared. Life in Hell was horrible, but it was better to be dealing out the torment than to be receiving it.

Jetrel shuddered, despite the searing heat, and tried to push the image of his own scorched and screaming face from his mind. He couldn't end up like that. He couldn't fail. He had to keep himself focused and do whatever he must to find the key. Nothing would stop him, and no one would get in his way. Who knows, maybe after he found the key, he would hunt down the angel that Heaven had sent and drag it back to Hell with him. Surely, the Master would give him an even greater reward if he returned to Hell with the key of the Abyss as well as one of God's pets in tow. The gift of tormenting an angel was one that the Master would surely cherish, and the benefits for the one who gave it to him would be substantial.

Jetrel stood and stretched. He sheathed his sword and headed back into the maze of tunnels. His departure time was approaching, and he still had a few loose ends to tie up before he headed to Earth. He had to make sure he had every possible advantage. He would only get one shot to prove his worth and he had to make it count.

CHAPTER 3 - RAIEL

Raiel lay on the ground, shivering against the cold concrete. He forced his twitching muscles to work long enough to roll himself onto his back, but it took great effort. He looked up at the few stars visible in the sky. Ordinarily, it would have been a sight he would witness with awe, but the pounding in his head and the knots in his stomach were overpowering anything else he might have felt. Even the painful cramping of his muscles and the cold night air were no more than minor nuisances in comparison. The air was heavy with moisture and smelled worse than anything he had ever experienced.

How can anyone live in this awful place? Raiel thought. He tried to sit up, and after several failed attempts, managed to work himself into the sitting position. Fireworks began exploding behind his eyes, and everything around him started to spin. He fought the urge to vomit and waited for the feeling of vertigo to pass.

After several painful minutes, Raiel felt steady enough to open his eyes again. He was sitting naked in a dark alley amidst garbage and small, scummy puddles of water. Seeing the water made him realize how thirsty he was, but nothing could make him drink what was in those puddles; the smell alone was enough to ward him off.

Raiel stood slowly, wobbling as if drunk. He stumbled to the closest wall and fell against it. The coarse brick tore flesh from his shoulder, but be barely noticed. All his focus was on trying to stay upright. He leaned heavily against the wall until another bout of vertigo passed and he was able to open his eyes again. His breath came out in heavy gasps, blowing clouds of steam into the cold night air. Surely nothing could be worth this amount of suffering. He cursed himself for ever agreeing to undertake this mission and wondered why the other angels seemed to speak so highly of Earth and its inhabitants. From what he had seen so far, there was little worth saving here, and he prayed that everything would become easier once his body adjusted to its new form.

When he felt that his legs would accept his weight, Raiel took a few uneasy steps toward the street. He moved cautiously, uncertain whether he could trust his legs. With a little difficulty, he managed to avoid the puddles, potholes, and garbage as he traversed the alley. By the time he reached the street, his legs were feeling stronger and his steps were becoming more confident.

Raiel stepped out of the alley and into the light. He looked up and down the street, trying to decide where he should go next. There were very few people out at this time of night, for which he was thankful. A nude angel staggering down the sidewalk was just the sort of thing people tended to notice. He turned and stumbled along, not having any particular destination in mind. Catching his reflection, he stopped in front of a storefront window and stared at the man looking back.

He looked as he did in Heaven—for the most part. He was about six feet tall with a muscular build. His hair was a deep golden blond and neatly trimmed. He had no facial hair and almost no body hair either. His skin was flawless, as was everything else on his body. His vivid blue eyes were clear and attentive. The only things missing were his wings, and the sight of himself without them made him feel less than whole. He didn't think he would have felt any different if he had looked at his reflection and realized his arms were missing. He knew that his wings would return once he was back in Heaven, but he would have given anything to have them back at that moment.

A young couple walked past him and he turned to watch them. They were staring openly and keeping as much distance between themselves and him as they could without actually walking in the street. Raiel watched them go and decided that he should be moving on as well. He continued down the street, trying to stick to the shadows when he could.

After traveling several blocks, he stopped to rest in an alley. The simple act of walking was enough to exhaust him. The sickness that had followed his materialization on Earth was much worse than he had thought it would be. The elder angels had warned him about it, but nothing they'd said could have prepared him for experiencing it firsthand. He sat down on the cold concrete and shivered. He needed some clothing and food but had no idea where to find either. It was late, and nowhere appeared to be open for business—not that it mattered since he had no money and no idea how to get any.

When the cold concrete became too much, Raiel stood slowly and started walking again. Quietly, he began praying for an opportunity to present itself before he succumbed to the cold and exhaustion. He traveled several more blocks and was getting ready to rest again when he saw a storefront window that caught his attention. There were several plastic men and women inside, each one dressed in a different outfit. It was hard to believe that this bizarre clothing was something humans would actually wear, but since this was his first trip to Earth, he had to assume that it was.

He stared at the clothing for several minutes, trying to decide what he should do. He needed clothing, but didn't want to resort to theft. He debated for several more minutes before walking into the alley beside the store and returning with a brick. He needed clothes, and this seemed to be the only way to get them. He regretted what he was about to do, but surely God would understand his dilemma and forgive him; after all, it was necessary to accomplish his mission.

Raiel took a quick look around before throwing the brick at the window. The glass shattered and an alarm began to blare from somewhere inside. He walked up to the window, trying his best to use his toes to push the glass from in front of him. He reached in, grabbed the figure that looked closest to his size, and pulled it from its stand. He turned back to the alley and walked toward it. When he was clear of the glass, he ran into the alley, stripping the clothes off the plastic man as he went. When he had its clothes and shoes off, he tossed it aside and ran from the alley, away from the persistent store alarm.

He ran for several more blocks until he felt that stopping would be relatively safe. He had been exhausted, but the adrenaline rush had given him a second wind.

Raiel slipped on the dark denim jeans and the red button-up shirt. The mannequin had been wearing a black tie with it, but after looking it over, Raiel tossed it to the side. He wasn't sure what it was for and decided he really didn't need it anyway. He sat down on the concrete to pull the glass fragments from his feet before putting on the socks and shoes. His feet were severely cut up, but he healed quickly. Within a few hours, the wounds would be gone, leaving no evidence of ever having been there. He couldn't wait that long for them to heal, so he pulled the socks on over his bleeding feet and then slipped them into the shoes. He winced in pain as he stood and slipped the soft, white leather jacket on.

Raiel walked out of the shadows and back onto the streets. He looked at himself in the reflection of another shop window and smiled. He didn't know the fashions on Earth, but if this was what was on display, it should work. They were a little large, but not enough to bother him. After seeing himself in the new clothes, he decided that he looked pretty good, even without the wings.

Raiel turned from the window and considered his next move. The pounding in his head had subsided considerably, and the knot in his stomach had vanished completely. What was left was a dull ache, which he assumed was hunger. He needed to find some food, but without money, he didn't have many options. He looked around the deserted street and wondered how he was supposed to get along on Earth when he had been provided with nothing. He'd been left to fend for himself in a strange new place and he didn't know how to do that. He had acquired clothing, but didn't want to push his luck by stealing again unless he had no other choice. Even once felt like too much, though it had been easier than he'd thought it would be.

With little else to do, Raiel once again started walking, hoping that he would be led toward a solution to his problem. He knew that he needed to be searching for the key, but his headache and the rumbling in his stomach made it hard to concentrate on anything else. He needed to find something to eat and a place to rest before starting his search.

CHAPTER 4 - JETREL

Jetrel opened his eyes and then quickly closed them again. He didn't know where he was or what had happened. He assumed that he'd made it to Earth since he didn't feel the suffocating heat or smell the familiar smoke and sulfur he knew from Hell. He wanted to open his eyes and look around, but the pounding in his head made it difficult. There seemed to be pain everywhere, which made him nervous about moving. He knew that he could be injured on Earth and thought that he could have broken bones or something worse.

"Are you alright?" a female voice asked. Jetrel flinched at the sound, causing the pain in his head to intensify. Now he definitely knew he wasn't in Hell since no one there cared if you were alright or not.

"Not really, but I think I'll live, if that's what you mean."

"What's wrong?"

"Nothing," Jetrel said.

"What happened to your clothes?" the woman asked.

"I don't know," Jetrel said. He was getting irritated with this woman and her questions. If he could have moved, he would have punched her in her stupid face. If he had his sword, he would have shut her up for good. He made himself sit up, causing the world to start spinning until he thought he was going to puke. He steadied himself and waited for the feeling to pass, still aware of the woman watching him.

"Are you sure you're alright?" the woman asked. "I could call someone for you if you'd like."

"I said I'm fine! Now if you're not gone by the time I get up, I'll cut your dirty whore's tongue from your mouth." Jetrel heard the woman gasp and managed to open his eyes just in time to see the old woman rounding the corner of the alley. He smiled and pushed himself up. He stood slowly but was unsure on his feet. He hoped that all people on Earth were as much fun as that woman was. He just wished he could have seen the look on her face before she ran off.

Once he managed to gain his bearings, Jetrel looked around at the alley he was in and tried to figure out what he was going to do next. He took some shaky steps toward the street before bracing himself against a dumpster. The other demons had told him that he would be in pain after arriving on Earth, but this was way more than he had expected.

After steadying himself, Jetrel continued toward the street, squinting as he stepped into the streetlight. Once his eyes adjusted, he looked around and saw that the streets were relatively deserted. There were a few women hanging out on street corners; most of them were dressed in very little. He wondered if one of these hookers was the woman who had approached him. He doubted it since none of them was old enough, but he still smiled about it before heading down the street.

Jetrel continued walking, ignoring the stares of those he passed. He stopped outside a bar and stared at the neon signs softly glowing in the window. He was amazed at how beautiful they were. After spending millions of years in a place devoid of any type of beauty, he couldn't believe how moved he was by so simple an object. If simple colored lights could awe him so, he couldn't wait to experience the truly great things Earth had to offer.

Jetrel shook himself from his stupor and walked into the alley beside the bar to wait. Fortunately, he didn't have to wait long. He was leaning against the brick wall, nearly halfway down the alley when a drunken biker rounded the corner. He was most likely heading for his motorcycle to drive home, or perhaps he had walked to the bar. Either way, it didn't matter; Jetrel was about to get what he needed.

"Hi, friend," Jetrel said. He tried to sound as pleasant as he could, not wanting to scare his target away or cause him to soil himself.

"Wh-who are you?" the drunk asked. He stopped and looked Jetrel up and down for a few moments before he realized what was wrong with him. "You're naked."

"Yes I am, but I'm about to rectify that." Jetrel stepped toward the drunk, who stumbled back and fell on his ass. He was a pretty big guy and close to Jetrel's height. The clothes might be a little bit baggy on him, but that didn't matter much; at least he would be dressed. He could always find better clothing later.

The drunken man sat on the cold concrete in a daze, which made it easy for Jetrel to step up and punch him across the jaw. The drunk fell backward with a heavy thud and didn't stir. He was still breathing, but unconscious. Jetrel knelt down and stripped him of his clothing as swiftly as possible, leaving the tattered boxers on him. He thought the jeans would be more comfortable with the underwear on, but couldn't bring himself to wear them. He started to get up, then thought about it and stripped the boxers off the biker anyway. He wouldn't wear them, but figured it would be funnier when the man woke up.

Jetrel walked to the back of the alley and put on the faded black Sturgis tee shirt, blue jeans, socks, and boots. He then finished off the outfit by putting on the heavy black leather jacket, complete with plenty of useless buckles and snaps. Across the back of the coat, an eagle spread its wings and clutched a tattered American flag. The phrase "Ride Free, Live Free" was displayed in a gentle arc beneath the eagle. He wasn't sure how necessary the jacket would be for most people, other than to act as a fashion statement, but he was freezing. After the searing temperatures in Hell, he could just as well have been in the arctic.

After dressing, he turned and headed back toward the street. He would have to find different clothing soon. These clothes smelled of sweat and beer. The grungy outfit made his skin feel as if there were things crawling across it, and he wasn't entirely sure that there weren't. That could wait, though. Right now, he needed to find something to eat and someplace to sleep. Both of these he could purchase using the money and credit cards in the biker's wallet, which was attached to his jeans by a heavy silver chain. He knew he needed to be searching for the key, but he would have to take care of himself first. There would be plenty of time to find it after a hot shower and some food.

CHAPTER 5 - FATHER STEPHENS

Father Stephens stood up from his recliner and carried his dishes into the kitchen. He placed them into the sink and returned to the dining room. He sat back in his recliner and picked up the newspaper. He skimmed through it, reading a few random articles that caught his eye. He had mixed feelings about the news. It seemed like most of the stories were about violence and hatred all around the world. He sometimes questioned why he still subscribed to the paper in the first place. He debated about cancelling his subscription but knew that he wouldn't. Even though the news was often depressing, he would rather know what was going on in the world than live in ignorance as so many others did.

He finished reading the paper and began his nightly ritual of preparing for sleep. As he went through his routine, an uneasy feeling had started to creep over him. He wasn't sure why it had started. He had been reading Revelations, which sometimes gave him an uneasy feeling, but it had never been like this. This had been an anxious feeling—the same feeling he got when he had to fly but worse somehow. He'd felt like he had to go somewhere unpleasant and was dreading it, except that he wasn't going anywhere. The only place he had planned on going was to the store the next day to get a few groceries. That was hardly a cause for concern. He went the store at least once a week to pick up what he needed.

Once Father Stephens was ready for bed, he couldn't fall asleep. The feeling of unease and fear continued to build, and he couldn't push it from his mind. He tossed and turned for a while before getting up and making himself some hot tea. He turned the TV on and watched an infomercial for a while, not really taking in any of it. His mind began going over everything he had done over the past few weeks and the upcoming things that he needed to do. None of it seemed important or anything he should be worried about. The feeling was driving him mad, but he didn't know what to do about it.

When the infomercial was over, Father Stephens turned the TV off. He sat in his black leather recliner and finished his tea in silence. He set his teacup on the end table next to the recliner, flipped the leg rest up, leaned back, and stared at the rough-textured ceiling until he slipped into an uneasy sleep.

Father Stephens slid so easily into dreaming that he wasn't even aware it had happened. Inside his dream, he woke to the sound of an explosion. The sound caused him to sit up, his heart pounding heavily in his chest. He stood and walked to the front door, slowly opened it, and stepped outside.

The sky was a deep crimson, and white lightning flashed from the black clouds. He started to shiver in spite of the incredible heat but continued walking into the yard with his eyes turned upward. When he reached the sidewalk next to the street, he turned around and looked back at his house.

In the sky above the house, a demon dressed in white hovered across from an angel dressed in black. Their wings were held open, catching the updrafts brought on by the approaching storm. The angel and demon watched each other, neither making a move toward the other. Then lightning spread across the sky, followed closely by an explosion of thunder that made Father Stephens press his hands to his ears. As if the thunder was their cue, the angel and demon lunged at each other, their clashing swords throwing sparks across the sky. The sparks crashed to the ground like meteors, setting trees and buildings aflame. The battle continued, and more meteors battered the Earth, but Father Stephens ignored them.

The angel and demon continued their battle, oblivious to the damage they were causing. Father Stephens' feeling of dread continued to build as he tried to decide whom he wanted to win. It seemed that no matter which of them won, the Earth was doomed.

Then both of them fell back momentarily before lunging forward again, each trying to deliver the killing blow. As the swords landed, there was an immense flash of light, and Father Stephens looked away, shielding his eyes with his arms. When the light had faded, he looked up and saw that the land all around was barren and burnt. Hideously mutated forms of animals wandered the Earth, seemingly lost and without purpose.

Father Stephens felt something tugging at his black robe and looked down. A horribly disfigured person was clawing at his leg, gurgling desperately from deep within his throat. The father gasped and tried to step back from the creature, but his path was blocked. He looked around and realized that he was surrounded by these mutated creatures that had once been human. They moaned and cried out unintelligibly, the act of speaking lost to them. Their eyes seemed to be pleading for help, or possibly death. He felt that death would be the best help these poor souls could receive. He tried to pull away from the hands that grasped his clothing, but he had nowhere to go. The wretched creatures began to wail as they pulled him beneath their writhing mass.

Father Stephens woke, the wailing from his dream replaced by the scream coming from his throat. He made himself stop screaming and wiped the sweat from his balding head. He smoothed out what little gray hair he had left and took a deep breath. His pajamas were soaked and clinging to him. He stood, shaking visibly. He went to the bathroom, stripped off his pajamas, and took a nice warm shower, letting the water wash over him until the shaking stopped. Once he calmed down, he washed himself and got out.

After drying himself and getting dressed, he felt a deep and sudden urge to go to the church to pray. Ordinarily, he would have just prayed at home, but he didn't feel like that would be sufficient. He needed to be in the church, surrounded by the old building's musty smell, mixed with the lemon wood polish used for dusting the pews. It was a comforting, familiar smell. He also wanted to be surrounded by the crosses, Bibles, and comforting images scattered throughout the church.

Father Stephens dressed quickly and got into his car. He was shivering, even though it was a warm night. He drove quickly to the church and rushed to the basement door in the back. He unlocked it, ducked inside, and relocked the door. He walked up the stairs from the basement of the church and stepped into the church proper. He looked across the rows of pews before heading toward the altar. He was breathing heavily as he reached the front of the church, so he sat on one of the choir chairs until he recovered his breath. He was getting too old and too fat to be running around the church in the middle of the night, especially when he didn't know the reason for it.

He rested a moment and then sighed and forced himself to stand. He turned to face the large cross hanging on the wall above the altar and fell to his knees on the red carpet. He closed his eyes and started to pray. His prayer continued through the night and into the morning. When he finally opened his eyes and looked up, he realized that the feeling of dread had dulled significantly. It was still there, but now he felt that he could manage to sleep. He stood up and left the church, knowing that whatever was coming, he would have God to look to for guidance. And that thought calmed him more than anything else.

CHAPTER 6 - LYDIA

Vivian twirled around the brass pole, making love to it. She was selling fantasies and the market was good. She slid slowly down the pole and onto the floor. She stretched out and rolled onto her back, running her hands seductively across her well-oiled body. She rolled to her knees and shook her head in time to the pounding bass, sending her dark hair whipping in all directions. She slid her hands up to her bare breasts and squeezed them roughly, nearly to the point of pain. She licked her dark red lips and looked into the crowd of men around the stage, trying to make eye contact with as many as she could. She had to try to make them notice her above all the other dancers. The competition was brutal, and she needed to draw as much attention to herself as she could.

On stage, her full name was "Vicious Vivian," and she performed five nights a week at the Eden's Shadow Gentleman's Club, but never for private parties. When she wasn't on stage, she was known as Lydia Jacobs, but that wasn't the name that made her the money; it was the one she used on her college financial aid forms. She was twenty-two and an aspiring journalist—at least that's what she told herself and her parents, who had no idea that Vivian was even a part of their daughter's life.

The song ended and Vivian stood and headed off stage, picking up the stray dollars as she went. She was done for the night and intended to go home and crash. Stripping didn't take a lot of time, but it did take a lot out of a person. It was all worth it, though—at least in her eyes. After all, she had managed to make nearly $200 tonight, and it had been a slow night. If the lap dances were really coming in, it could be as high as $500 or more, depending on how many women were dancing.

Vivian slid off her G-string and headed for the shower backstage to wash the oil off. She had been in school most of the day, and then it was off to work for the evening—a pretty routine day for her, but it still managed to wear her out. She stepped into the shower, letting the warm water run over her long, black hair and down her tanned, toned body. When not in school or at the club, she spent a lot of her time working out. It had almost become an obsession for her—one she thought was acceptable. It wasn't smoking or drinking, but it did give her a rush. Plus it was good for her and her work.

Vivian mustered her resolve and made herself move so she could finish her shower and head home. She lived in a small apartment by herself and definitely preferred it to living in the dorms. She had done that for her first three years of college, and then she'd decided that she needed her space. She couldn't be around the partying, drinking, and all the other distractions of dorm life since she was taking eighteen credit hours and working at least five evenings a week—sometimes more if the club had someone call in.

Vivian finished showering; when she stepped onto the cold tile floor, she was plain old Lydia again. After drying herself off, she walked to her locker and got her clothes. She dressed quickly, wanting to get home. It was a chilly night, and she wasn't looking forward to the walk. She was saving money to get a car, but after rent, utilities, and such, she didn't have a lot left to put into savings. She made good money, but a lot of it went to pay off the debts she had built up when she'd first started college. She was making progress on the credit cards, which helped to keep the creditors off her back, but she still had a ways to go.

She went to check in with the manager before leaving for the night. He was a jerk, but the money made it easier to put up with him. Money often had a way of making people more tolerant of one another. As for Mike, he saw the girls who worked for him as little more than property. Sometimes Lydia and the other girls joked that because of how badly he treated them, he must be gay. Most other club managers were notorious for sleeping with the strippers. In some clubs, you couldn't even become a dancer unless you slept with the manager first—not that any of them wanted to sleep with the fat, greasy bastard.

After a few words with him, she managed to slip away and head for the back door. She grabbed her jacket and stepped outside, putting it on as she went. She looked around the alley, shivering in the cold night air. Her wet hair only seemed to magnify the cold, and Lydia wished that she'd had the foresight to bring a hat, or at least a jacket with a hood. Her mother had often told her that she needed to think more and daydream less, and at times like this, Lydia was apt to agree with her.

She knew her parents worried about her being on her own in the city. They tried to talk her out of moving into her own apartment, but she wouldn't be dissuaded. They told her that she would be much safer on campus where they had security and there were lots of other students around. She'd told her parents it didn't matter because every year there were rapes and other crimes right on campus amidst the security and all the students. This information didn't help to ease her parents' worries, but it did take some of the fight out of them. She supposed that since she was an only child, they were a little overprotective.

Lydia shivered as she started down the alley toward her apartment. She wanted nothing more than to get home, have a quick bite to eat, and head to bed.

As she got about halfway to her apartment, Lydia realized she was being followed. She desperately wanted to turn to see who was following her and if there was more than one of them. She debated running, but figured that would draw them to her that much quicker. As it was, they didn't know that she aware of their presence. She weighed her options, hoping to think of a place that she could go where there would be other people, and then she could call the police. But just as she had the thought, a man stepped in front of her, blocking her way. She tried to step back, but he caught her jacket and pulled her to him. He clamped his hand tightly over her mouth and turned her around. He wrapped his arm around her neck, holding her against him.

Now Lydia was able to see the other two men who had been following her. She immediately recognized them from the club and wondered why it had taken her so long to realize they'd been there. She had always thought of herself as an observant person, but today her powers of observation had failed her.

"Hey, 'Vicious Vivian,' where your whips at?" one of the men asked. He smiled at her, showing his few remaining teeth. He was a skinny white guy who smelled as if he hadn't showered in weeks. He was pale and his face was full of sores, which was a clear sign of his meth habit. His hair, which was the only neat thing about him, was cut in a high and tight military style, which stood out from the rest of his grungy exterior.

The man next to him was Mexican. His hygiene and skin were better, but not by much. His hair was a greasy, overgrown tangle that nearly covered his eyes. He stood shorter than the other two, but had a much harder look to him. This was a man who had seen and been involved in a lot of bad things in his life.

Lydia had only gotten the briefest of glances at the man holding her in a painful choke hold, but he fit in perfectly with his friends—especially his odor and the fact that most of his clothing had probably come from a dumpster. He was white and the largest of the three both in height and breadth. His hair looked almost like the Mexican's, except that it was blond instead of dark brown.

"So what are we going to do with her?" the Mexican asked.

"I think we can figure out something to pass the time," his friend said. "She makes her living being a whore, so she should be used to doing the things we've got planned."

The large man holding her shoved her forward and she stumbled into his two friends. They caught her, clamping her mouth quickly before she could scream. They pulled her jacket off and roughly tore the blouse from her. She hadn't bothered to put a bra on since she was heading home, and now her breasts were exposed, her nipples hard in the cold night air.

"Look at that!" the Mexican said. "Look how excited she is." He reached up and pinched her left nipple painfully hard. Tears squeezed from her closed eyes as she struggled uselessly to break free from their grasp.

The largest of the three unbuttoned her jeans, unzipped them, and yanked them off her, taking her shoes with them. She screamed into the hand of the man with the buzz cut as she desperately prayed for help. She doubted anyone would come, but there was nothing else she could do. The man with the buzz cut kicked her hard in the back of her right leg, and she dropped to her knees. She looked around and saw that all three men were standing around her with their penises in their hands.

"Now," the big guy said, "why don't you get to work? And don't try anything funny, 'cause this is happening whether you're alive or not. If you'd rather it be while you're alive, then you'd better not scream. And if I feel a single tooth scrape me while you're giving me head, I'll break your fuckin' neck."

Lydia figured that they'd kill her no matter what she did, and she almost preferred to be dead when they raped her. Her body felt weak, and she didn't think she would be able to move even if she wanted to.

CHAPTER 7 - RAIEL

Raiel's search for food and shelter had been going poorly. He had been walking the streets for several hours, asking everyone he saw for help. Most people just ignored him, and a few snapped comments such as, "Get a fucking job!"

He was starting to wonder what was so great about Earth. The people were rude and only concerned about what was happening in their own lives. They couldn't be bothered to help another person in need. And weren't these the people he had been sent here to save?

Raiel stopped outside of an old apartment building and sat down on the broken steps. The old concrete held in the cold and seemed to amplify it, but he didn't care. He had been walking for a long time and still hadn't recovered from his trip to Earth. He was hungry, tired, and sore, but his feet hurt the worst of all. He had never worn shoes before, and they were rubbing his feet raw. He suspected that they were a little too small for him. He pulled the shoes off and rubbed his feet, completely unaware of the group of young men coming up the sidewalk toward him.

"Look here, guys," one of them said. "He's pretty well dressed for this neighborhood, ain't he?"

"A little bit," another one said. "Maybe we should help him out with that."

Raiel looked up and saw that there were five young guys standing at the foot of the stairs, all looking intently at him. They were all dressed in clothes that were much too large for them, with bright red bandanas tied to various parts of their bodies. A couple of them were black, a couple Hispanic, and one was a short white guy. Raiel realized that they had gotten the drop on him, making him feel incredibly stupid. They were no more than kids, and he doubted they had any sort of military or stealth training. Plus they were all wearing gold chains and metal charms, which would have made silent movement nearly impossible. No, he had simply been too lax. He supposed some of it could be attributed to his condition, but it was mostly that he hadn't expected any trouble from these humans.

"I don't want any trouble," Raiel said, as he got up. "I was just stopping to rest my feet for a few minutes; now I'll be on my way."

"Not so fast," the short white guy said. "There's an issue of the toll. We're going to need those fancy clothes and shoes of yours if you want to pass."

"What? That's ridiculous, these are my—" Raiel's sentence was stopped short as one of the black guys stepped up and hit him. Raiel stumbled backwards, falling against the steps. He reached up and felt the blood running from his nose. He looked at the guys in front of him for a moment before leaping at them.

The young guys spread out, apparently sensing the attack coming. Raiel's fist connected hard to the face of one of the black guys, producing a very satisfying crunching sound. He spun and drove his elbow into the short white guy's throat and then kicked the other black guy in the stomach. Raiel tried to turn to face the other two attackers, but was struck across the back of the head. He dropped to his hands and knees, and the group of men surrounded him and proceeded to beat him into unconsciousness.

Raiel didn't know how long he had been lying on the cold ground, but it was still dark when he came to, so it couldn't have been more than a few hours. He sat up slowly and realized that he had been thrown into a dumpster. All his clothes were gone, except for his jeans. The jeans had been taken partway off, but were still there. Maybe when they saw that he wasn't wearing underwear, they decided to leave them. It was a small blessing, but he would take any he could get.

So far, everything Raiel had seen of Earth had been horrible. He was starting to believe that all humans were selfish, mean, and cold. They went about their lives, intent on helping only themselves. Even their charity was only given to those who seemed worthwhile to them and usually only near the holidays. He had witnessed this over and over again while watching them from Heaven. If someone who was dying approached them on the street, how many would actually help, and how many others would turn a blind eye and let someone else deal with the problem? They were very frustrating, but God loved them unconditionally. How this was possible, he didn't know.

Raiel struggled to stand, his body aching once again. He pulled his pants up and fastened them before climbing out of the dumpster. He limped from the alley. His face and his body were bloody and starting to bruise. There were many large gashes all over his body. Most of them had stopped bleeding, but he had a feeling that any kind of exertion on his part could make them start up again.

Raiel turned and looked out at the street on which he was standing. It was pretty much like any of the other streets he had seen, but it seemed to have a much darker, uglier look to it now. Hidden danger seemed to lurk around every corner, and he felt as if everyone was out to get him. It wasn't a pleasant feeling, but he hoped it would help him achieve his goals. It would definitely help keep him on the lookout for trouble. He didn't intend to be caught unawares again.

He turned and headed back down the street, seeing very few people around at that time of the night. He didn't know where he was going, but he knew he needed to find a hospital, clinic, or someplace he'd get some medical attention. His wounds weren't life threatening, but they were bad enough to require some sort of attention. He needed to find a phone or someone who would actually stop long enough to direct him to the hospital. Maybe he would be able to get something to eat there and finally get some rest. He needed both desperately if he hoped to have any chance of finding the key.

It took him a lot longer to move around the city than it had before. The longer he walked, the more his body seemed to ache, and he knew that there was a lot of swelling. He stopped quite often to rest, praying that he would find help soon.

Raiel stopped in an alleyway to rest and saw several people at the other end. He leaned his back against the cold stone and watched. There were three guys, all surrounding a woman. One of them had a hold of her while the other two looked on. They seemed to be speaking, but he couldn't make out what they were saying from that distance. Then, the larger guy, who had been holding her, shoved her to the two other guys, who grabbed her and started pulling her clothes off. Raiel stood, took one more glance at them, and then continued on down the street. It wasn't his problem, and he didn't have any more time to waste dealing with these people. Let them worry about themselves. That's what they were best at anyway.

CHAPTER 8 - JETREL

Jetrel approached a small twenty-four-hour diner and went inside. It wasn't the nicest or cleanest place, but it would have to do. The smell of the food was incredible, and it made his stomach start to rumble even louder. He walked to a booth and sat down. He only waited for a minute before the waitress arrived to take his order. He ordered a beer and a cheeseburger. He wasn't really sure what either tasted like, but he had heard that they were popular on Earth, so he figured they must be pretty good.

After the waitress left, he sat and watched the few patrons in the diner. Most of them appeared to be working-class people, probably lower class judging from their attire—not that he was in a position to talk; he looked like a cookie-cutter biker, complete with the Sturgis shirt and black leather jacket, and all his clothing smelled of body odor, beer, and cigarette smoke. He would be glad when he could ditch them, or at least find somewhere to wash them. Even if people didn't look their best all the time, they could at least wash their clothes. Everything on this planet had its own putrid odor, and he seemed to be the only one to notice it. Maybe everyone had grown accustomed to their own stench. The sooner he could find the key and get back to Hell, the better.

While he was lost in his daydream, the waitress arrived and delivered the food and drink to him. It was very fast service, but it also looked to be pretty slow in there that night. Most of the patrons seemed to be drinking coffee and chatting, probably talking about something stupid going on in their pathetic lives.

Jetrel picked up the cheeseburger and sniffed it. It didn't smell bad, which was a welcome change. He looked it over before finally taking a bite. It was delicious, and he started to wolf it down. He had no idea that food could be so wonderful. He swallowed, and then looked at his glass of beer, which he noticed was bubbling. He dipped his finger in it, but it wasn't hot; it was actually very cold. He took a drink and nearly spat it across the table. It was vile. Why would it be so popular? He set the glass down and flagged down the waitress.

"Is everything alright?" the woman asked.

"No," Jetrel said. "This beer is awful."

"Is it flat?" the woman asked. Jetrel then noticed her name tag, which read Jolene.

"I don't know, but would it be possible to get something else?"

"Sure, what do you want?" Jolene asked.

"I don't know, but something that tastes better than this. Just pick something."

Jolene eyed him suspiciously for a moment, but must have decided that he wasn't trying to pull something over on her. She turned and left the table, and Jetrel started eating the fries on his plate. They were good, but nothing like the cheeseburger.

"I hope a pop works for you," Jolene said. She set a glass of black liquid down and then left. He cautiously took a sip and then started drinking it down greedily. It was even better than the burger, which was saying a lot. It was sweet, but had a pretty good kick to it. The ice in it was too cold, but he ignored it and emptied the glass. He set the glass down and belched loudly. Nearly everyone in the diner turned and looked at him but quickly resumed their conversations. Their tolerance for rude behavior seemed to be relatively high.

Jetrel set the glass down, and Jolene came to take it for a refill.

"No ice, please," Jetrel said. After she went behind the counter to fill his glass, he paused for a moment and wondered why he had said "please." It had been thousands, if not millions, of years since he had used that word. It must have been the food and drink. They seemed to fill him with a sort of giddy energy. It was something he hadn't felt before, but it felt good.

After finishing his food and several more glasses of pop, Jetrel paid the bill and left the diner. He was still tired, but it wasn't such an overwhelming exhaustion anymore. He had asked Jolene where he could find a hotel, and she'd pointed him in the direction of one a few blocks down the road. Once he had gotten a good rest, he thought he would head back to the diner to eat again before starting his search for the key. The thought filled him with an odd excitement. It was weird that he would get so excited about eating, but he had never eaten before and he couldn't wait to do it again.

After traveling several blocks toward the hotel, Jetrel noticed a group of people standing in an alley. He almost walked past them but noticed a nearly nude woman on her knees at the center of the group. Jetrel watched the horrified woman and felt his desires stirring. It had been a pretty good day so far, and he knew that it could get even better. He looked around and found an old piece of two-by-four amidst the debris scattered around. It was dry and rather weak, but he hoped it would be strong enough to do some damage. He picked it up and quietly approached the group of men.

"Now," the big guy said, "why don't you get to work? And don't try anything funny, 'cause this is happening whether you're alive or not. If you'd rather it be while you're alive, then you'd better not scream. And if I feel a single tooth scrape me while you're giving me head, I'll break your fuckin' neck," Jetrel heard the man with his back to him say. He lifted the board up and broke it across the back of the guy's neck, dropping him immediately.

"What the...?" the little white guy across from him said. "We're gonna fucking kill you."

"Give it your best shot," Jetrel said. He lunged at the guy, driving the jagged end of the two-by-four into his gut. The guy doubled over and fell over backwards, while the little Mexican guy pulled a knife from inside his jacket and came after him.

Jetrel stepped back, easily avoiding the first slash of the knife. The Mexican advanced, swinging in wide arcs which Jetrel dodged. It was evident that this guy had never had any training in the proper use of weapons. Luckily, Jetrel had, and he also knew how to turn them against their owners. At the next swipe of the knife, Jetrel caught the guy's wrist and twisted it. The Mexican grunted but didn't let go of the knife. Jetrel threw his weight forward, turning the hand with the knife and driving its blade into the man's abdomen. He gasped and stared at the knife protruding from his stomach. The blood seemed to rush from his face to his wound, and he started screaming. Jetrel flinched at the sudden noise and slammed his fist into the guy's face, cutting the screams short.

Jetrel looked around at the three unconscious bodies, proud of his victory. It had been an easy battle, but a battle nonetheless. He turned back to claim his reward, but before he knew what was happening, the woman threw her arms around his waist. Jetrel looked down at the sobbing woman in surprise, not knowing what to do next. He was prepared to have his way with her and had expected fear and groveling. She evidently saw him as a savior instead of the larger predator eliminating the weaker ones. Now he found himself wavering in his resolve, but he wasn't sure why. She looked up at him. Her eyes were a stunning golden brown, swimming beneath the tears. She was breathtaking, but that wasn't why he hesitated.

In Hell, torture was a daily part of life and one that Jetrel loved. Now, the simple act of a woman crying and thanking him over and over again left him feeling confused. Maybe it was because in Hell no one ever thanked you or saw you as anything other than a monster. Now someone was seeing him as something more, and it felt nice to be thought of in that way, even though it was a lie. He was a monster, and if the young woman soaking his shirt with tears knew what he had been planning to do to her, she would have thought so too.

"Stop it," Jetrel said. He pulled the woman's arms from around him and stepped away from her.

"What?"

"Don't be thanking me and making me out to be some sort of hero, lady."

"My name's Lydia."

"I don't care. Now gather up your clothes and get out of here."

"Why are you acting like this?" Lydia asked.

"Acting like what? I just don't want to make a big deal out of this. Now get out of here." Jetrel turned and left the alley quickly, not looking back to see whether or not Lydia was leaving. It didn't matter anyway; whatever happened to her now was her problem. He had his own to worry about.

CHAPTER 9 - LYDIA

Lydia wasted no time in gathering her clothes. As she dressed, she watched the three men on the ground in case any of them started to stir. After she finished dressing, she dug through her purse until she found her cell phone. She called 911 and then waited at the end of the alley for the cops to arrive. After the cops showed up, they had her fill out a report and had all three of the men taken to the hospital to have their injuries checked out before they were taken to jail. She didn't know or really care how badly they were injured. If they lived, fine; if they died, she wouldn't shed any tears over it.

Once the police had everything they needed from her, she was free to go on her way. They had asked for all the details about the attack, and she'd told them everything she could think of and given them a description of the man who had saved her. She asked if he was in trouble and they told her that he wasn't; they just wanted to talk to him to get a statement. They said he sounded like a real hero, but they were a little curious about why he would save her and then leave her alone in the alley. She had been curious about that too, and she promised them that if she ever saw him again, she would tell him that the cops needed a statement from him.

After the cops dropped her off at her apartment, she went inside and sat on her couch, shivering. She'd had a close call and it was really starting to get to her. She had always thought of herself as a strong woman—a woman who could handle any situation she came across. In the end, though, she had been powerless to protect herself. If that guy in the biker jacket hadn't shown up when he had, she would have been raped, probably killed, and then possibly tossed in a dumpster, where her body might never have been found, or her naked body could have been left on display in the alley for everyone to see.

Lydia tried to turn her thoughts to better things, but her brain only wanted to play the frightening game of "What If...?" She decided to run a hot bath to try to draw the chill from her body and hopefully relax her overactive imagination.

Once the bathtub was full, Lydia slowly stepped into it. The water was nearly hot enough to burn her, and she had to move slowly to keep from being scalded. Once she managed to lie back, her mind started to lose focus on what had almost happened, and she began to focus on the mystery man who had saved her. He was about six feet tall and athletic. He had long black hair and eyes so dark brown that they looked almost black. He was cute in the way that only bad boys could be, but he also had their attitude. She had dealt with plenty of them in her lifetime and knew their tempers well.

She reached up and turned on the shower radio, mainly because she craved the noise. After what had happened, her apartment seemed too quiet and too dark. She then settled back into the tub, trying to think of something that the guy in the biker jacket had said or done that would give her some sort of clue as to who he was; but nothing came to her. He hadn't even told her his name after she had told him hers. That had been odd, but not as odd as his reaction to her gratitude.

Lydia sighed and started to wash herself. She didn't feel like sitting in the tub anymore, and it wasn't helping her to feel better anyway. When she ran her hand over her left nipple, she cringed. It was swollen and bruised from being so brutally pinched, and she once again started thinking about how differently the whole situation could have turned out.

Once Lydia was washed and out of the tub, she put on her robe and checked her front door again to make sure it was locked. She had checked it a few dozen times now and wondered if she would become obsessive–compulsive about it. Once in a while, she would double-check the lock in the past, but she had never checked it this many times before. After checking the lock again, she curled up on the couch and turned on the TV but didn't really watch it. She tried to clear her thoughts but failed again.

She wondered how she would ever be able to go to work again after this. She would always be wondering if the guys giving her money were planning to follow her after work to rape and kill her. Her profession wasn't known for dealing with the highest class of people, but she had always thought that it couldn't happen to her. Maybe she should quit the job and find one that was a little safer. The only problem was that the other jobs didn't pay nearly as well as this one did, and she didn't think she would be able to deal with such an extreme pay cut. That left her with little choice other than to stay at the club.

She got up and turned off the TV, her restlessness getting the better of her. She went to the kitchen, took a couple of sleeping pills, and headed for bed after checking the front door lock again. She then took a chair and propped the back of it under the doorknob for good measure. Once the door was secure, she crawled into bed, leaving the bathroom light on for security. She didn't know whether or not she would be able to sleep, but she figured she'd try. She only hoped that her dreams wouldn't betray her the way her waking imagination had.

CHAPTER 10 - FATHER STEPHENS

Father Stephens sat inside the confessional and listened to those coming in to confess their sins. At least he *tried* to listen, but found himself slipping into daydreams more and more frequently. At first, he thought it was from a lack of sleep, but he didn't feel tired. In fact, he'd woken up with more energy than he'd ever remembered having. He seemed to be overflowing with energy, and he used it all to his advantage. He spent the whole morning cleaning his house, rearranging his furniture, going through piles of papers on his desk, filing away those he wanted to keep, and throwing the rest away. He then went to the church, where he worked on sermons and cleaned up his office. When he started doing confessions, the energy that had been so abundant earlier left him as suddenly as it had entered him.

Now he struggled to stay focused on what was being said to him, but just couldn't seem to do it. The spirit was willing, but the flesh was weak, as his mother used to say when she felt tired.

As he slipped back into a daydream, he started seeing images swimming before his eyes. He saw a man leaving work early and driving to a house that wasn't his. He reached the house and went in, kissing the woman inside deeply. It was the kind of kiss only two lovers can share—very private and personal. He somehow knew that this woman wasn't the man's wife and that this situation had been going on for quite some time.

They would meet a couple times per week if they could, but it was oftentimes much less than that. It drove them crazy that they couldn't meet more often, but the man didn't want his wife to begin to suspect anything. The woman he was now embracing wanted the man to leave his wife, but somehow she knew that he wouldn't do it. He loved his wife and kids, but the sex had become all too predictable and infrequent for him.

Then he saw the man leaving his mistress's house and getting into his car. He sprayed a little cologne on and tidied himself up before leaving. Once he got home, he checked himself quickly in the mirror to make sure there were no telltale signs of his earlier activities, and then he went into the house. He was greeted by a quick peck on the lips from his wife and three kids, all of whom were trying to tell him about their day. He spent some time with his kids and then they all had supper together. He helped his kids with their homework, and then he tucked them into bed. He spent time talking with his wife while they watched TV in bed before going to sleep.

The man in his vision loved both of his lives, but for entirely different reasons. Together, these lives completed him and gave him something neither of them alone could give him. He felt guilty about leading this double life, but he didn't know what to do about it. If he gave up either one, he would be giving up something he truly felt he needed in his life, but he didn't think he could go on living the lie for much longer.

"That's why I came to you today, Father. I need some guidance and advice."

Father Stephens woke from his daydream, finally hearing the man next to him talking. He hadn't really heard what the man had been saying, but somehow he knew that this was the man he had seen in his vision. It was a man who was torn and looking for answers.

"Well," Father Stephens said, "marriage is a sacred bond, which should not be thrown away purely to fulfill your physical desire. Those desires fade with time, and what you will be left with is what you and your wife already have. I suggest that the two of you talk about your physical relationship and possibly see a marriage counselor. Just don't throw everything away for a temporary fix to a long-term problem."

The silence from the booth next to him was all the answer he needed. He knew that was what the man needed to hear, but didn't know how he knew. He supposed it went along with the vision he'd had earlier, but he didn't know why he'd had the vision. Was it to help him with the confession, or was there some other deeper reason for it? And would he keep getting them?

Father Stephens continued his confessions, each producing similar visions and the same results. He gave a lot of good advice that day—perfect advice actually. He was able to know exactly what each person needed to hear to ease their minds and help them take a step toward ending their sinful ways. He began to see the visions as a blessing from God, and he intended to use them for as long as God saw fit to bless him.

That evening when he left the church, Father Stephens felt as if he'd been hit by a truck. He was exhausted and his whole body felt sore. His head was pounding more severely than he had ever experienced. He was starting to believe that the gift he had been given was killing him from the inside out. He needed to avoid people as much as he could, and he certainly wasn't going to do any more confessions for a while. He doubted that the human body was meant to see things like that for too long. He had probably just overexerted himself and needed to try to gain some sort of control over his gift.

When he got home, he took several aspirin and tried to lie down in his bedroom with the lights out; but each time his head pounded, it looked like a flash was going off in front of his eyes. He was on the verge of vomiting and was really starting to become concerned. What if these visions had given him a brain tumor? Or what if they were being caused by a brain tumor? He had seen a movie like that before and wondered if it was even possible—maybe not, but somehow when you're alone in the dark and not feeling well, bad thoughts creep into your mind. It was something common to a lot of people, but no matter how much you tell yourself you're being silly, the ideas keep flowing in.

Father Stephens thought maybe he should get up and watch some TV to take his mind off everything he had been going through over the past several days; but he decided that he wouldn't feel better no matter what he did, so he might as well stay in bed and try to relax.

Just as he thought the headache was starting to subside, another vision started. In this one, a young woman was sinking in a dark pit of tar and struggling to free herself. Two men stood beside her, one on each side. One was dressed in white, the other in black. Both of these men were close enough to save her, but she had to reach out to one of them. If she chose the wrong one, he would let her sink. The right one would pull her free, but somehow he knew that even then she wouldn't be safe. It would only mean that she had a fighting chance to survive the upcoming trials.

He tried to get a good look at the woman and the two men, but their faces were indistinct. He had to try to find this woman and help her. This was why he had been given the gift; of this he was now certain. He didn't know who the woman was or why she was so important, but he would do everything in his power to help her. God had shown him the path he needed to take. All he had to do was take the first step.

Then, as suddenly as it started, the vision stopped, leaving his head pounding even worse than before. He wanted to find out more about the woman, but had no idea where to start. All he had was a feeling about her, but he hoped that he would recognize her if he saw her. Until then, all he could do was sleep and try to avoid people. That way, he could keep his head clear until he needed to use the gift again. God had sent the visions and would send more when the time was right.

CHAPTER 11 - RAIEL

After the attack, Raiel began to search for a hospital. He managed to follow street signs and make his way to the emergency room. Once there, the hospital staff took him in and began their examination and questions. They wanted to know everything about the incident, which he willingly told them. Then the police showed up to ask all the same questions and to get a description of the guys. Raiel gave them the best description he could, but it wasn't very good. All humans look alike to him.

Then the questions turned to him and who he was. He did the best he could to lie his way through the interrogation and keep his answers straight. He told them he was from Australia and was in the United States to visit relatives. He said that all his paperwork had been stolen by the kids that attacked him. The cops didn't seemed to buy the story, but they kept their mouths shut and wrote down everything he said. He also told them that he had been on the way to his cousin's house when he got lost and that he had been trying to find a street name that he recognized when he ran into the group of guys that had assaulted and robbed him.

As he talked to the police, a doctor came into the room and begun stitching up the large wounds on his body. He watched, fascinated, as she ran the needle repeatedly through his skin; he was amazed that he couldn't feel it. He continued with his story as he watched, but he still noticed the looks that the cops were giving each other at a few key points. Once the cops were finished, they left, saying they would contact the relevant people to try to verify his story. Until then, he would be left under guard and would be unable to leave his room. If he needed anything, he would have to call the nurse.

After the cops left, the doctor continued sewing his wounds, which she then bandaged. She gave him some more pills and ensured that someone brought him some food. By most people's standards, the food would have been lousy, but to Raiel, it was incredible. He wolfed down everything as quickly as he could and then took his pills. He then pushed the empty tray away and lay back on his bed to watch TV.

Raiel lay in his hospital bed, flipping through the endless channels on the TV that hung from the wall. He knew about TV but didn't know much about the shows. Some of them seemed like they might be interesting, but since he knew so little about current customs in the world, much of what the characters said was lost on him. All he knew was that the world was a violent place and that a lot of the violence could be seen on TV. He'd experienced some of that violence firsthand and had the wounds to prove it.

Raiel wondered how long it would take the pills to kick in. The doctor had told him that it was something to help him sleep, even though he didn't think he needed anything. After the day he'd had and the meal he had just eaten, he didn't think it would take much to put him out. He continued aimlessly flipping through channels, occasionally stopping to watch something interesting that caught his eye. When his eyes eventually started to droop, he put the remote down and allowed himself to drift off to sleep.

Raiel had no idea how long he had slept, but when he woke up, the nurse was standing next to him, giving him a sponge bath. He felt rather uncomfortable, so he closed his eyes again and pretended to go back to sleep. He would have told her to stop, but he desperately needed the bath since he was covered in dirt and dried blood.

Once the nurse was finished, Raiel sat up and looked around. He didn't know what time he had gone to sleep, but it felt like a long time had passed. He felt much better, and his wounds looked much better too. As an angel, his wounds healed rather quickly, which was something he hoped the nurses hadn't noticed. But even if they hadn't, it wouldn't be long before someone noticed his amazing recovery. Plus, he needed to get out of there before the cops realized his story was made up and came back to question him again. He needed to get started on his mission and didn't have time to deal with suspicious cops.

Raiel pushed the call button and waited for the nurse to arrive. When she showed up, he asked about getting something to eat, and she told him she would find something and have it for him in a little bit. He watched some more TV while he waited for the food to arrive, and he started trying to figure out a way to get out of the hospital without causing too much of a scene. If he'd still had his wings, he could have gotten out through the window, but he didn't, and since he was on the third floor of the hospital, he ruled out the window option.

He was still working through several plans in his head when the nurse came in with a tray of food. As with the previous meal, Raiel wolfed it down. He didn't know when he would get to eat again, and he wanted to take advantage of it while he could.

Once he finished eating, he pulled the IV out of his arm and stood up. He was still a little wobbly, but he steadied himself against the bed until his legs were stable enough to allow him to walk. Then he went to the door and listened; he heard nothing out of the ordinary. He figured there was still a guard on the other side of the door, which was the biggest problem he had to deal with. He needed to get rid of the guard and find some clothes. He couldn't walk around wearing a hospital gown. At least it had been nighttime when he'd arrived on Earth naked, and he'd been able to stay in the shadows, but now it was daytime and sunny.

Raiel went over to his IV stand and removed the IV bottle. He picked up the stand and used it to smash the glass in the window. The glass shattered, and a moment later, the door flew open and the policeman who had been guarding his room stepped in. He had his gun drawn, but Raiel was too quick. He swung the IV stand, catching the guard's hand and sending the gun sliding across the polished tile floor. He ran to the door and pushed it shut, hopefully before anyone realized something was going on. He turned back to the cop and got punched across the jaw. He took a step back, startled at the guard's speed. He evidently wasn't one of the regular cops—slow of mind and soft of body. This might be a tougher fight than he had anticipated.

The cop stepped up and took another swing at Raiel, who barely managed to dodge the blow. Raiel dodged another swing before he was finally able to get in one of his own, but it landed hard. The cop was a little stunned but wasn't out of the fight. Raiel hit him again, hoping to get this finished before a nurse or doctor came in. He needed to get out of the hospital as quickly as he could. The cop swung at him and barely connected as Raiel tried to back out of the way. Raiel grabbed the cop and threw him across the room. The cop hit the bed and turned back to Raiel, who hit him again. Raiel grabbed him by the hair and slammed his head against the metal armrest of the bed, knocking him out.

Raiel grabbed the cop and wrestled him onto the bed. Then he started stripping off the cop's clothes and putting them on. A cop uniform wasn't the most discreet thing he could have worn, but he had very few options at that point. Once he was dressed in the cop's uniform, he pulled the covers up over the cop's head. He then went to the window and pulled the curtains. He pushed the few glass shards that had gotten inside behind the wardrobe and hid the broken IV stand in the bathroom. He then put on the cop's hat and pulled it low over his face before stepping out of the room.

Once in the hallway, he saw the cop's coat hanging on the back of a chair just outside the door. He took it and put it on, casually watching to see if anyone had noticed him. From what he could see, no one had, but that didn't mean he was out of the woods. He still had to get out of the hospital without being recognized, which he hoped wouldn't be too difficult with all the people around.

Raiel walked through the hospital, following the signs leading to the exit. He kept his head down as much as he could, trying to avoid eye contact with anyone. A couple of nurses asked if they could help him find something, but he just ignored them and kept walking.

Just as he was beginning to get frustrated with the maze of hallways, he saw an exit door and headed for it. Once he passed through the door, he finally breathed a sigh of relief. That ordeal was over with. Now all he needed to do was find a different set of clothing and lie low. The police would surely be searching for him once they found out what he had done. He would need to stay out of sight as much as he could while looking for the key.

Raiel noticed a police car sitting in the parking lot and assumed that it belonged to the officer who had been guarding him. He considered trying to take it, but he had never driven before and figured it would cause more problems than it would solve, so he dismissed the idea. Instead, he started walking down the street, trying to decide his next move.

CHAPTER 12 - JETREL

Jetrel knelt over the bathtub, trying to wash his clothing with the little bottles of shampoo provided by the motel. He had checked in the previous night shortly after he'd inadvertently saved Lydia from being raped. He had been hoping to have her for himself and it was driving him crazy thinking about what had happened. Was he losing his touch? Or was it simply that the new emotions he was having were overwhelming him? Before he left Hell, he was told that he would experience new emotions on Earth and that they could confuse him. He had been expecting that to happen, but had been totally unprepared for how strong they would be.

When he finished washing and rinsing his clothes, Jetrel wrung them out and hung them in the room to dry. He was about to wash the jacket, when he noticed the tag that said "dry-clean only." He wasn't sure what dry cleaning was, but he understood the dry part of it. So he took a damp washcloth instead and wiped it down, hoping it was dry enough. Then he dried it off with a towel and hung it up. The coat hadn't smelled nearly as bad as the other clothes, and he figured he would find better clothing soon anyway; so if it was ruined, it wouldn't be too big of a loss.

With his clothes hung out to dry and his stomach still satisfied, he decided to get some rest before going out again. He lay down on the bed and stared at the ceiling, with his arms behind his head. He started thinking about the only thing that he had been able to think of since the previous night, which was Lydia. In Hell, he would have had his way with her and then broken her neck for no other reason than to hear it snap. In Hell, he used to pull women from the flames all the time. He would have his way with them and then after he was done, he'd send them to an even worse torment in the lower levels. That way, they would suffer even more, and he wouldn't have to be with the same woman more than once. There were plenty of gorgeous women in Hell, so he always had enough from which to choose. It seemed that the prettier the woman was on Earth, the more likely she was to do sinful things.

Jetrel tried to push those thoughts from his head. What he needed to focus on now was finding the key. The sooner he found it and returned to Hell, the sooner everything would be back to normal. Then this whole lapse in judgment would be nothing more than a distant memory. When he had safely returned to Hell, he would watch for Lydia in case she wound up there. Then he would be free to take her as his own and subject her to the worst torments he could think of for causing his resolve to waver.

With a plan now firmly set in his mind, he finally managed to clear his thoughts and drift off to sleep. When he woke up, he would start his search for the key, which was his ticket off this planet.

Jetrel slept soundly and deeply. He had been concerned about outside noises, but his exhaustion kept him from hearing anything. He didn't know how long he had slept, but his clothes were dry and it was nighttime again. He guessed that it had been about twelve hours, give or take. His body was sore and stiff, but other than that, he felt great. He got out of bed and took a shower, running the hot water at nearly scalding.

Once Jetrel was showered and dressed, he turned his key in to the front desk and headed back toward the little café where he had eaten the first night he'd arrived. He knew that other places would have good food too, but he had really enjoyed that place and wanted to try it again.

On the way back to the diner, he passed the alley where he had saved Lydia. He gave it a quick glance, determined not to stop, but he found himself stopping anyway. He walked down the alley to where the incident had happened. There was little trace that anything had occurred—not even any blood. The only thing he saw were some splinters from the board he had broken over the back of the big guy's head. Even just standing there, he felt his emotions begin to overwhelm him. He had helped someone instead of hurting them, which was something new to him. The last time he had done anything to help humanity was when he had been an angel under God's command, back before Lucifer attempted to overthrow Heaven. That had been a long time ago, but he was starting to remember how it felt and it sickened him.

Jetrel was reluctant to leave the alley, but he forced himself to turn around. Then he heard a sound, which made him turn back. He scanned the alley until he saw the source of the noise. A small dog, not much more than a puppy by the looks of it, was rooting through a pile of garbage, looking for food. It was mostly white with a few spots of brown. Its hair was greasy and dirty, but its tail was wagging as if it didn't have a care in the world. Jetrel watched it for a minute before whistling to it. It lifted its head and looked at him, tail still wagging. It seemed to be familiar with people, so it must not have been a stray all its life. It had probably been dumped off somewhere or had run away.

The dog cocked its head at Jetrel and turned to face him. It had one large brown spot that covered its eye, and its ears hung down at the side of its head. He whistled again, and the dog trotted over to him excitedly. It wasn't scared of people, which made Jetrel wonder why it hadn't yet been picked up by the dogcatcher or a kind family.

The dog looked up at Jetrel expectantly as it approached him. When it was close enough, Jetrel kicked the puppy into the brick wall. The puppy yipped once in surprise before it hit the wall and tumbled onto the ground in a heap. Jetrel smiled and walked over to the puppy's corpse. He kicked it into the pile of garbage that it had been sniffing at and then kicked more garbage on top of the body.

Jetrel turned and walked out of the alley, whistling happily as he went. Now he was starting to feel more like his old self. Maybe now he could finally put the whole incident with Lydia behind him and be able to concentrate on his mission; but first, he wanted to eat again.

The diner was nearly empty and Jetrel sat in the same booth in which he had sat before. The waitress came over and gave him the menu. He looked it over before ordering a steak and a pop. Once again, he didn't have to wait long for his food, and he ate it greedily when it arrived. The steak wasn't as good as the cheeseburger he'd had before, but it wasn't bad. It was a little dry, but the pop was just as good as he remembered, and it helped him wash down the steak. Once he was done and had paid, he stepped outside onto the sidewalk and looked up at the night sky. It was a cool night, and the stars almost seemed to be magnified. He stared at them for a minute before looking back to the street. When he did, he saw something that made his heart skip into his throat.

Across the street, Lydia was walking quickly toward the alley where he had saved her before. Then, just as quickly as it had been restored, his good mood came crashing back down. He watched her as she walked, wrapped in her coat, nervously throwing glances over her shoulder.

Jetrel watched her walk away from him, his mind a jumble of questions. She didn't seem to have noticed him. He fully intended to let her go on her way, but then his legs started following after her almost on their own. He started out walking, but soon started picking up speed to catch up with her.

Jetrel soon found himself running, knowing he would catch sight of her at any minute. When he didn't, he stopped to catch his breath and gain his bearings. He stared down the street ahead of him, wondering where she had gone to. Had she turned off somewhere behind him before he could catch up to her? He was about to turn around and go back when he realized something was happening to him. He had a funny sort of humming feeling going on in his head; it was barely more than a tickle. He knew that an angel was close by. He had been told that he would be able to sense angels when they got close. Whenever he came within several yards of another demon or an angel, he would feel a funny sort of buzzing in the back of his head. The only one it could have been was the angel God had sent to find the key.

Jetrel started to turn around when something struck him across the back of the head. His mind reeled as his vision went dark and he slipped into unconsciousness.

CHAPTER 13 - LYDIA

Lydia awoke the next morning feeling a little better than before she had fallen asleep. As she got up to go take a shower, her back screamed in protest. Her couch wasn't meant to be slept on, and her back always paid for it the next day. She stretched as best she could and rubbed the knots in her back until they softened up a bit. She then padded along the carpet on her bare feet and went into the bathroom. She decided to run a bath and soak in the hot water to see if it would help relax the muscles in her back.

While she ran the water in the bathtub, she went into the kitchen to make some coffee. Coffee always seemed to make her feel better, and she couldn't wake up without it. After the coffeemaker was going, she went back in to use the bathroom before she got in the tub. She waited till the tub was full before flushing the toilet, or else the water would turn scalding. She then went back to the kitchen to get her coffee and brought her cup into the bathroom. She slid into the hot water, which was once again on the verge of being too hot to bear. She sat in the water, letting her body adjust to it, and sipped her coffee. So far, her day had been like all the others; there'd been only vague thoughts in her mind of the incident from the night before.

After her bath and first cup of coffee, Lydia climbed from the tub. She was feeling better; the pain in her back had lessened to a dull ache, and she felt more awake and vibrant. She put on her robe and got another cup of coffee while she watched TV. She watched the news, almost expecting to see something about the incident the previous night, but she didn't. It didn't surprise her too much. In a big city like the one in which she lived, much worse crimes happened every night. If she had been raped and killed, she might have made it on the news. She shuddered at the thought and wrapped the robe even more tightly around herself.

Lydia spent the morning lounging around the apartment before getting ready for her classes that afternoon. It was one of the few mornings that she could afford herself that luxury, which was only because she'd blown off her morning class.

When she moved the chair from in front of the door and left her apartment, she was feeling pretty good.

Her classes that afternoon were pretty boring, as usual, and she once again found herself wondering why she was in school in the first place. She could make a lot of money at the club and wouldn't have to deal with school. She told herself that, but deep down, she knew she couldn't be a stripper forever. Eventually, she would get older and would be replaced by younger, perkier girls. Then she would be stuck having to do some menial minimum-wage job, and she didn't want to do that either. And if she stayed at the club, she would be dealing with the same old pervs every day. As it was now, she was able to tell herself that it wouldn't last forever, which made it easier to deal with them. The biggest reason to get away from the club was because it would break her mother's heart if she found out that Lydia was working there.

After her classes were over for the day, Lydia had some time before she had to be at work. She went to the gym on campus and worked out for a couple of hours. By the time she got to the club, she was almost feeling like her old self.

Upon arriving at the club, Lydia showered and put on her costume. "Vicious Vivian" was a hardcore dominatrix complete with black leather and whips. Often during her shows, she would spank men from the audience and if not them, then one of the other strippers. It was all part of the role she played. Most of the women had their own individual roles. There was the naughty nurse, the catholic school girl, the French maid, among other such characters. One time, they even had a woman who dressed up like a nun, which turned out to be very popular with the clientele. Usually, they chose their own roles, and they were each supposed to be unique. On a few occasions, they would have two of the same characters go out on stage and perform together, but for the most part, the rule was to have only one of each.

When Vivian was dressed, she went to the DJ and let him know that she was there and when she was going on. From there, he would know what music she was supposed to have and when to start it. All she had to do now was wait for her music.

Vivian's entrance onto the stage was pretty much like normal. She stepped through the curtain and cracked her whip, which she had become really good at. Then she started her routine, which was going along flawlessly until she looked out into the crowd and saw all those men staring back at her. She froze and just stared into the crowd. Any of these men could be thinking the same thing that those guys had been thinking the previous night. They could be planning to follow her home after work to rape and kill her. Then another terrifying thought came to her: What if the guys who had followed her the previous night were out of jail and had come back to finish what they had started?

"Come on! Let's see some skin!" someone yelled from the crowd.

Vivian was jarred from her thoughts and continued with her routine. For the rest of the night, she was a little stiffer than usual with her moves and was very aware of the men in the crowd, but she managed to finish her routine.

When she was done and showered, Lydia sat in the dressing room by herself. She had nearly freaked out on stage and it had her worried. If she couldn't dance, she would lose her major source of income. She was getting caught up on her bills, but she still wanted to get a car and save some money for after she graduated. She had so much of her life planned out already, and a lot of it was dependent upon the money that dancing brought in.

Lydia decided she should get up and head home, but she found that she didn't want to. She had started out telling herself that she didn't want to go out with wet hair, but she knew that it was a lie. She always went out into the cold with wet hair, and it had never been an issue before. She was scared, plain and simple. She had walked home through that alley hundreds of times, and nothing had ever happened to her—until the previous night. Now because of that one incident, she was terrified to leave the safety of the club and was scared of the patrons she counted on for money.

Finally, after deciding that she couldn't sit in the dressing room all night making excuses, Lydia made herself get up and head home. She put on her coat and walked to the door. Her teeth were chattering, but it wasn't because of the cold. She opened the door, stuck her head out, and looked around thoroughly before she stepped outside.

Lydia started down the alley, looking over her shoulder frequently, swearing that she heard footsteps behind her. She started out walking, but soon picked up her pace. She just wanted to get home as quickly as she could. Her mind was playing tricks on her and she was terrified of everything around her.

Lydia was trying to calm herself down when she saw a man across the street in front of the City Stop Diner. When she first saw him, he was looking up at the sky, but she could see his silhouette back lit against the diner windows. She watched him from the corner of her eye and saw him look over at her.

He stared for a few moments before he started walking after her.

Lydia started walking even faster, her heart pounding hard against her ribcage. She felt sure that it would give out at any moment and she would die of fright right there on the sidewalk. She wanted to run, but figured that the man would start running after her. She still had a slight jump on him and she needed to use it while she could.

When she felt like the man was far enough behind her so that he wouldn't see her, she turned off onto a side street. She sprinted down the street, nearly running into a man who stepped out in front of her. She wanted to scream, but somehow managed to stop herself.

The man in front of her was wearing a police uniform and seemed just as shocked as she was.

"Whoa!" the officer said. "What seems to be the problem?"

"There's a man following me; I was just trying to lose him."

"Well, let's step out of the street and you can tell me what happened." The officer, whose nametag said "Officer Stillman," took a hold of her arm and pulled her into the alley. Lydia followed reluctantly, looking over her shoulder as she went.

Lydia told the officer the story as quickly as she could, and when she finished, he nodded. He told her to wait while he went to check it out, and then he left her alone in the alley. She was nervous as she waited for Officer Stillman to return, but she waited patiently.

It was several long minutes before the officer returned, but when he did, he looked disappointed.

"What happened?" Lydia asked.

"Well, I saw the guy, but he managed to get away. I wish I could have caught him for you, but he's gone for now."

"Thank you for trying," Lydia said. "I just hope he doesn't come back."

"Well, for now, how about I take you to the diner nearby and buy you a cup of coffee? You look like you could use someone to talk to."

Lydia smiled at him and nodded. She felt a lot safer with him around, and she could use something to take her mind off everything that had happened. Plus he looked close to her age and he was really cute.

"I think a cup of coffee would be nice," Lydia said. "My name's Lydia, by the way."

"It's nice to meet you, Lydia. My name's Raiel."

CHAPTER 14 - RAIEL

Raiel moved through the streets, trying to avoid people as much as he could. If someone thought he was a real cop and asked for his help, or another cop recognized him as a fake, then his whole mission could be in danger. He stuck to the alleys and kept his head down at all times. On the few occasions that someone said hi to him, he would simply nod and continue on his way. He kept walking until he found a dead-end alley with two large dumpsters in it. He chased out the bum he found sleeping there and sat hidden behind the dumpsters until darkness fell.

Once the streetlights came on, Raiel came out from behind the dumpsters and headed for the small diner that he had passed earlier. He went in and sat down. The waitress took his order without so much as a second look at him. He had found some cash in the cop's wallet that he would use to buy his supper, and he would keep whatever was left. He felt guilty about using money that wasn't his, but he had little choice; it was either use the money or go hungry. Besides, the cop would probably be reimbursed for everything he lost. He didn't know if that was true or not, but it made him feel better about keeping the money.

When his food arrived, he ate it as quickly as he could, feeling like all eyes in the diner were on him. When he looked up, though, everyone was involved in their own conversations, and no one was looking in his direction at all. He finished his meal, paid for it, and headed for the door.

Once Raiel was outside again, he felt a little better. He started walking again, trusting his intuition to take him in the direction of the key. He hadn't been walking long when he realized that he was in the same neighborhood he had been in the other night when he'd been attacked. He looked around, anxiously searching for the guys who had jumped him, but he saw no one. He started to go on his way, but something stopped him. He wanted to see those guys again. He wanted to give them a little dose of what they had given him.

Raiel walked around the neighborhood until he found a thrift store where he used the cop's money to pick up some new clothes and a backpack. He then took his new clothes into a nearby alley and changed. He folded the cop's uniform and put it into the backpack in case he needed it later. Then he walked around the neighborhood, looking to exact his revenge.

It took several hours of wandering the streets before he saw the group of guys he had been looking for. It didn't look like any of them were wearing the clothes that they had taken from him, but they could have easily sold them or stashed them somewhere. Either way, he knew that these were the guys, so he followed them for a little bit.

They walked up and down the streets, seeming to patrol the neighborhood. After a while, they stopped and sat on the steps outside of a building not far from where they had found him. They took out cigarettes and passed them around, each person taking one and lighting it. They sat around smoking and talking. Occasionally, they all would laugh at something one of them said, or make comments about people's cars or about the people themselves as they drove by. Raiel hung back and watched, but no one in the group noticed. They were too busy smoking and feeling superior in their own little world—a world he was about to tear down around them.

Raiel picked up a decent-sized rock, stepped out from his hiding spot, and threw it at one of the guys. The rock found its target and thumped off his head. The guy fell to his knees, spouting every swear word he had ever learned. Even from that distance, Raiel could see blood flowing from between his fingers. He had apparently put a pretty good gash in the guy's head.

Raiel stood in plain view, allowing the rest of the group to get a good look at him before he stepped back into the alley and pulled the cop's pistol from its holster. He knew what guns were and had spent a lot of time trying to figure out how it worked as he'd hidden behind the dumpster all afternoon. It was actually pretty simple to use once you knew how. All he had to do now was keep a level head and take the time to aim.

Raiel didn't have long to wait before the first of the group rounded the corner, drawing a gun. The rest of the group followed right behind, each one with a gun.

The guy in the lead lifted his gun at Raiel, but Raiel was ready. He fired once and the guy's head snapped backward as a small hole appeared in his forehead. The back of the man's skull exploded outward, spraying everyone behind him with blood and brains. None of the others even slowed as their companion fell, a trait he would have found admirable in any military unit. They were completely focused on their mission and would stop for nothing. There would be time for mourning later, if they survived.

The next one in line started to lift his gun, but Raiel shot him in the chest before he had a chance to aim. The third guy was the one he had hit with a rock. He held his left hand against the wound on his head and held his gun in his bloody right hand. He brought it up to fire, but it slipped from his grasp. He brought his left hand from his head to try to get a hold of the gun, but it bounced away from him. He turned to get it as Raiel fired, hitting him in the left shoulder. The kid screamed and fell, his gun forgotten.

The last two were lifting their guns to fire, but seeing their friends die seemed to take some of the energy out of their attack. They hesitated for just a second, but it was long enough for Raiel to put a bullet into each of their foreheads. They dropped heavily against the concrete, each producing a dull thud.

Raiel walked up to the guy he had hit with the rock; he was writhing on the ground. They stared at each other a few moments, before a look of recognition appeared on the guy's face.

"I know you," the guy said.

"I'm glad you remember me, because I haven't forgotten you."

"Look, man, we were only trying to protect our turf. It wasn't anything personal."

"You were trying to protect your turf from an unarmed man who had sat down to rest his feet? What kind of threat was I to you? What you're saying doesn't make sense. Besides, what makes this your turf? You're just trying to find a reason to hurt and kill people. You're nothing but scum and deserve to be wiped off the face of the Earth."

"Wait, man, please don't..." The guy's plea was cut short by the report of Raiel's gun. Blood splattered all over, covering Raiel head to toe. He had ruined his new clothes and would have to change back into the cop's uniform. He started toward the street, but stopped and turned back to the bodies. He went up to each of them and dug through their pockets until he found their wallets. He took whatever money they had and tossed the wallets aside. He had found a lot more money than he'd expected and assumed it was probably drug money. He didn't know for sure, but he figured that they were using it for something illegal, or had gotten it illegally. Either way, he would put it to good use. He also found a beautiful gold lighter in one of their pockets. He flipped the lid back and flicked his thumb across the flint as he had seen them do when they'd lit their cigarettes. The flame jumped to life, and Raiel watched it for a moment before snapping the lid closed and putting it in his pocket.

Raiel left the alley and started running down the sidewalk. The police would probably be there soon, and he needed to put some distance between himself and the crime scene. He ran to an old gas station he had seen while walking around the neighborhood. It was closed, but that didn't matter. He went around back to the door marked "MEN" and kicked it in. It took several tries before the door gave way, but when it did, he stepped inside and closed it the best he could. He stripped out of the bloodstained clothes and tossed them on top of the overflowing garbage can beneath the cracked porcelain sink. He turned the water on and washed himself off using the soap in the hand soap dispenser.

After washing himself in the sink and drying himself off with paper towels, he pulled the police uniform from the backpack. He hated to put it on again, but it was either this or walk around the city naked. He didn't plan on wearing it long anyway—just until he could find another store and pick up some real clothes again.

After putting the uniform on, Raiel stuck his head out the doorway and looked around. There was no one to see him, so he stepped out, leaving his bloody clothes and backpack in the bathroom.

Raiel started walking toward the thrift store, away from the crime scene. He tried to stick to the alleys as he usually did. He was leaving one of these alleys when he nearly got knocked over by a young woman.

"Whoa!" Raiel said. "What seems to be the problem?"

"There's a man following me; I was just trying to lose him," the woman said.

"Well, let's step out of the street and you can tell me what happened." Raiel took the woman's arm and led her into the alley. She told him her story, but Raiel was barely listening. He was starting to hear a low buzzing sound in the back of his mind, and he knew exactly what that meant. The demon was nearby.

Raiel told the woman to stay there while he checked things out, and he left the alley. As soon as he rounded the corner, he took off in a dead run, following the hum in the back of his head. As he rounded a corner, he saw the demon standing about ten yards in front of him. Its back was to him, so he drew the policeman's club from his belt and crept up behind it. He lifted the club above his head just as its head jerked up. It had apparently just realized he was there, but it was too late. Raiel brought the club crashing down across the back of the demon's skull, knocking it forward and into unconsciousness. That had been too easy. He wondered why the demon hadn't sensed him earlier, but he dismissed the thought. It didn't matter. The only thing that mattered was that he had been able to subdue the demon without it knowing he was there.

Raiel took the handcuffs off his belt and cuffed the demon's hands behind its back. He then dragged it into the alley, took its belt off, and used it to bind its feet. He found an old newspaper, wadded it up, and stuffed it into its mouth. Then he took a shoelace from its boot and tied it around the demon's head, securing the gag in place. He took the other shoelace off its other boot and hog-tied the demon. Then he hoisted it up and pushed it into the large dumpster in the alley. He thought about killing it, but he didn't want to risk getting blood on the uniform. Besides, the garbage truck would do it for him in a few hours. For right now, he had a woman in distress to attend to.

CHAPTER 15 - JETREL

When Jetrel came to, he didn't know where he was or how he'd gotten there. It was dark, and his head was pounding nearly as badly as it had been when he'd first arrived on Earth. He tried to move but couldn't. His hands and feet were bound behind his back. He didn't know what was in his mouth, but it tasted awful. He tried rolling around, but was covered in what he assumed by the smell was garbage.

Jetrel fought against the bindings but couldn't free himself. If he wasn't able to escape soon, he would be killed when the garbage truck emptied the dumpster. He weighed all his options, but none of them would help him. He could keep struggling or lie quietly and accept his fate. He chose to keep struggling, but the angel had tied him up expertly. Leave it to the angels to teach their recruits rope use and knot tying.

Jetrel heard the lid thump open against the side of the building. He tried to turn himself to see what was happening, but he couldn't. All his struggling had caused him to sink even further into the garbage. He didn't know how anyone would find him without digging through the filth. More than likely, someone was about to throw more garbage on top of him and bury him even further. He listened to the rustling of garbage and started moaning and wriggling around to try to draw the person's attention.

"What do we have here?" Jetrel heard someone say. "What are you doing in the dumpster?"

Jetrel felt someone climb into the dumpster beside him and start tugging on the ropes that were binding his hands and feet. He remained motionless to make it a little easier to untie the knots, but from the sound of the man's cursing, it still wasn't easy. The guy stopped working on the knots and untied the string around Jetrel's mouth with relative ease. Jetrel spat the newspaper out of his mouth and gagged, trying not to vomit until he could get some saliva flowing. The newspaper had dried his mouth out completely. He was having trouble swallowing—and more importantly, spitting—to help get the awful taste of dirty newspaper out of his mouth.

"Are you alright?" the man next to him asked.

"I've been better," Jetrel said. "Who are you?"

"My name's Samuel, but everyone calls me Sam. I was digging through the dumpster when I saw you wiggling around like a fish out of water. Usually when people are thrown into the dumpster, it's 'cause they're dead, but you're not. It's some world we live in, eh?"

"You said it," Jetrel agreed. "Do you have a knife or anything to cut the ropes with? They're starting to get a little uncomfortable."

"Yeah," Sam said, as if suddenly remembering. "I guess I do. Hang on a minute."

Jetrel tried to remain patient while Sam rummaged through his pockets. It took a while, but he eventually heard the click of a blade being opened. Then Sam started sawing at the bootlaces. The knife must have been incredibly dull, because it took a long time before he finally felt the string give way. Then Sam undid the belt from around Jetrel's legs.

"That's about all I can do for you right now," Sam said. "I don't have any way to get the handcuffs off."

"Help me up and I should be able to get out of here."

Sam helped Jetrel stand and turn around. Jetrel then worked his legs over the edge of the dumpster. Sam pushed his torso up until Jetrel slid out and onto the ground. Sam climbed out of the dumpster without the grace that Jetrel had. He clumsily threw his leg over and tried to slide the other over after it, but managed to slip and fall out onto the concrete. He lay there for a moment, before stumbling to his feet.

"Are you okay?" Jetrel asked.

"Yeah," Sam said, "happens all the time."

Jetrel looked at Sam, realizing for the first time that he was homeless. He had been saved by a bum, a fact that would have revolted him at any other time. Now, however, he was just glad to be out of the dumpster. He wouldn't have cared if he'd been saved by Jesus himself.

The bum managed to stand up with the help of the dumpster next to him. He was dressed in several layers of clothing, which may have been colored once, but were all now the same dusty gray. He wore old boots, a stocking hat, and a backpack, all of which were the same color as his clothing. Jetrel could say a lot about the man, but at least he was color coordinated. Even his face, the parts that weren't covered by his scruffy salt-and-pepper beard, was nearly the same dusty gray. The only bit of color on him was a gold crucifix that hung around his neck on a worn piece of string.

"Are you alright?" Sam asked.

"Yeah, except for the handcuffs, the splitting headache, and the nasty taste in my mouth."

"I think I can help you with those last two," Sam said. He reached into one of his coat pockets, pulled out a small bottle of whiskey, and offered it to Jetrel, who looked down at it and smiled.

"I'll take some of that, but you might have to help me out a little since my hands are still cuffed."

Sam looked at Jetrel for a moment before a look of understanding crossed his face. He took the cap off the bottle, put it to Jetrel's mouth, and tipped it up. Jetrel took several large swallows, holding the last to swish around his mouth. He swallowed the whiskey and felt the warmth move down his throat and spread through his stomach.

"Thanks," Jetrel said. Again, he thought it odd to be thanking someone for something he could just as easily have taken by force.

"No problem," Sam said. "Now let's go see if we can find someone who can get those handcuffs off."

Sam headed out of the alley and, with little other choice, Jetrel followed him. The two men walked through town, heading deeper into what was known by most people as the slums. Sam would occasionally stop in an alley or near a bridge and look around. There were several times when Jetrel almost asked him what he was looking for, but he decided to hold his tongue. He needed Sam's help, as little as he liked to admit it, and didn't want to distract him or cause him to lose focus.

Finally, Sam stopped near a bridge overpass and found the man for whom he'd been searching. Sam walked back to Jetrel, with the other man along in tow. The other guy was obviously homeless as well, but his clothing seemed to be in much better condition.

"This is my friend David," Sam said. "David, this is my new friend...ummm..."

"Jetrel. I would shake your hand, but mine are a little indisposed right now."

"Nice to meet you," David said. He walked around behind Jetrel, who was wary about letting the old man out of his sight, but he stood where he was. He doubted that there was much this old man could do to him, and so far, Sam hadn't given him any reason not to trust him—not that it mattered; mistrust was deeply ingrained into his personality.

David muttered something and Jetrel heard something jingling. Then he felt the old man's hands on his, fumbling at the handcuffs. After several seconds, he heard a click. The cuff on his right arm clicked open, followed soon by the left one. Jetrel rubbed at the raw skin of his wrists, as David came back around to stand by Sam. He had the handcuffs and tucked them into his coat pocket.

"Thank you, David," Jetrel said.

"David has all sorts of different keys," Sam volunteered. "He collects them."

"Do you have any keys I can have?" David asked.

Jetrel reached into his coat pocket, pulled out the key ring that had belonged to the coat's former owner, and tossed them to David, who snatched them greedily, his eyes lighting up like a child with a new toy. He turned and headed back toward the underpass while Sam came over to stand by Jetrel.

"Do you wanna go back to my place and have a drink?" Sam asked.

"Where's your place?"

"It's in an old steam tunnel under one of the buildings not too far from the dumpster where I found you."

"Probably not. I've got some things I've gotta take care of," Jetrel said.

"What kinds of things do you have to take care of?"

"First of all, I need to find some weapons in case someone tries to throw me in a dumpster again."

"I think I can help you there too," Sam said. "How about you take me to lunch and then I'll help you out with your weapon situation?"

"Okay," Jetrel said, smiling. "I think I can do that."

"Okay, that sounds good." Sam turned and started down the street. "I know of a good little place we can go."

CHAPTER 16 - RAIEL

Raiel and Lydia entered the diner and sat down together. They looked over the menus briefly before each ordered a cup of coffee and a piece of pie. Once the waitress had taken their orders, they sat in awkward silence. Finally, Lydia decided that it was up to her to start the conversation.

"Aren't you supposed to be on duty?"

"I was on duty earlier today," Raiel said. "I was just walking home when you tried to run me over."

"Sorry about that."

"Don't worry about it; you had good reason."

Lydia smiled at Raiel, who returned the smile. He had found her attractive outside, and now that he was seeing her in the light, he thought she was even more beautiful. He had been warned to avoid women while on Earth because they tended to distract from the mission. Plus, they came from separate worlds, so there could never be anything between them. But at that moment, none of that mattered. Raiel was intent on getting to know this woman better.

"So, what do you do for a living?" Raiel asked.

Lydia continued smiling, but now it felt forced. She hadn't even thought about what to say if he asked her that, and she was now at a loss for words. She hadn't had a serious relationship for such a long time that the topic of her occupation had never come up. Now she'd met a nice guy who'd tried to help her out, and she didn't want to tell him about her job. Plus he was a cop. What self-respecting cop would ever date a stripper?

"I'm a student right now," Lydia said. "I'm studying journalism, but my major changes almost daily." She hoped that she had avoided the question well enough to alleviate his curiosity.

Raiel nodded and took his coffee and pie as the waitress brought them over. Lydia smiled again—genuinely this time. She was glad he hadn't pushed the subject. Once he got to know her better, maybe she would bring it up. For right now, she thought it was better that he not know.

Raiel and Lydia sat and talked while they ate, but none of it was really important. It was typical first-date kinds of stuff, even though neither of them thought of it as a date. Lydia thought it was nice to sit and talk to a guy without him expecting something more from her. Raiel thought it was nice to be able to sit and eat. The fact that it was with a beautiful woman was an added benefit.

Once they finished at the diner, Raiel walked Lydia home. She was worried that the man who had been following her would be outside waiting, but Raiel assured her that he wouldn't be. He was happy that he had found the demon and been able to kill it. Now he was free to find the key at his leisure. Once he had the key and returned to Heaven, he was sure God would forgive him for the indiscretions he had committed so far. He couldn't have been the first angel sent to Earth who had sinned a bit.

Raiel left Lydia at her apartment door and, after getting her phone number, continued on his quest to find more suitable clothing. He had pressed his luck with the police uniform just about as far as he dared, and he wanted to be rid of it.

He walked around the town, not finding anyplace open where he could get new clothes. He started to debate whether or not he should steal another set of clothing when he happened upon a church. He saw the lights on and wondered if they would have something in the donation bin that he could use. They were for those in need and, at the moment, Raiel considered himself to be in need. Plus he hadn't done any praying since he'd arrived and thought that maybe it was time he did.

Raiel approached the small church with a strange sense of awe. It appeared to be nothing more than a regular church, but there was a sense of power coming from it that Raiel found odd. It was a feeling of goodness, but beneath it all, where he could barely sense it, was another feeling. It wasn't exactly one of evil—more like a sense of sorrow or mourning. It felt like the church was nothing more than a disguise—a way to hide something that someone wanted to keep secret.

When Raiel grasped the handle and opened the door, the only thing he saw was the inside of a small church. A man knelt at the front of the church, praying in front of the large cross that hung on the wall above him. He could only see the back of the man, but Raiel noticed that he was dressed in all black and was balding. The hair on the back and sides of his head was gray with a good mottling of white. Raiel assumed the man to be the priest of the church but wondered why he would be there so late.

"Excuse me, Father," Raiel said. "I don't mean to interrupt, but I saw the lights on and thought I would spend some time in prayer."

"That's no problem, my son. I couldn't sleep and decided to open the church and do some praying of my own." The priest stood and turned. He was a heavy man with a round and pleasant face. His brow was creased with worry lines and there were deep bags under his eyes. He looked at Raiel and his face lit up. He ran over to Raiel, looked closely at his face, and then reached out slowly and touched him, as if to make sure he were real.

"What are you doing, Father?"

"I am Father Stephens."

"Alright, and you can call me Raiel."

"I know who you are. You're an archangel sent to Earth in search of the key of the Abyss. I'm sorry to be rude, but I couldn't believe you were actually here. I just had to make sure you were real."

"How do you know who I am?"

"Lately, I know far more than I should," Father Stephens said. "I've developed a gift of sorts, which allows me to see people's pasts. It's been a great help to me in my ministering, but it causes severe migraines."

"So you knew who I was by seeing my past?" Raiel realized he had started sweating, despite the cool temperature in the church. If Father Stephens saw what he had done while on Earth, he would probably be cast out—except that he had greeted him warmly. If he had seen what Raiel had done, he wouldn't have given him such a warm reception.

"No, I only saw the golden glow around you and your wings. Your name and mission just came to me, but I can't see anything of your past."

"What do you mean? You can see my wings? I haven't had them since I arrived on Earth."

"Oh, you still have them," Father Stephens said. "It's just that they're in spiritual form on the astral plane. That way no one can see what you really are—except for me."

"Is that because you're supposed to help me?"

"I imagine it is. Why else would I have been given this gift?"

Raiel shrugged and reached out for Father Stephens. He placed his hands upon either side of his head and began mumbling a quick prayer. After several moments, Raiel stepped back and sat down in one of the wooden pews. His head was spinning, and he felt like the pie and coffee he'd eaten were on their way back up. He closed his eyes until the feeling started to pass, and then he opened them again. He looked up at Father Stephens, who was staring at several large, white feathers on the floor.

"Don't worry about those," Raiel said. "Those fall off my wings when I use my powers here on Earth. Apparently when they fall off, they become corporeal."

"What did you do to me?" Father Stephens asked. "My headache's completely gone and so is my arthritis. I feel better than I have in years."

"I just used my powers to remove the pain from your body, though I'm afraid it's not a permanent solution. Your arthritis is gone, but it will return slowly. As for your headache, it will return if you overuse your powers again, so I suggest you take it easy."

"Why did you lose feathers when you healed me?"

"As an angel, my body is composed of pure goodness and light. We call it Goldenlight, but it's not really anything tangible. When I use my powers on Earth, it saps me of this Goldenlight energy, and I lose part of my mass. The more energy I use, the more feathers I lose. If I use too much energy and lose all my feathers, it will start eating away at my body."

"Do the feathers grow back?"

"Eventually my body will absorb the Goldenlight it needs and regrow the missing feathers. It usually takes about as long as it would take a wound to heal. The bigger the wound, the longer it takes to heal."

"Well, thank you for ridding me of the pain, even if it's only for a short while," Father Stephens said. "Is there anything I can do for you?"

"Well, I could use some new clothes if you have something to spare. I also need to spend some time in prayer. I haven't had much of a chance since I arrived."

"I'll go and see if I can find you something to wear. Meanwhile, feel free to pray if you'd like."

"Thank you, Father," Raiel said. He watched Father Stephens go down the stairs to the basement, and then he knelt in front of the large cross behind the altar and stayed on his knees in prayer for nearly an hour before getting up. He turned around and saw Father Stephens sitting on the first pew with a pile of clothes.

"Are you alright?" Father Stephens asked.

"I'm fine. Why?"

"You just look a little upset. Anyway, I found you a bunch of clothes. If you'd like, we can go to the basement and you can try them on."

"Thank you, Father," Raiel said. He watched the priest go down the steps, and then he began to follow him to the basement. He was worried but didn't realize that it showed.

Evidently, Father Stephens saw it, but whether it was because of his powers or not, Raiel didn't know. All he knew was that he had been deep in prayer for over an hour, but no matter how hard he tried, he couldn't connect to Heaven. God wasn't listening.

CHAPTER 17 - LYDIA

Lydia walked into her apartment, feeling better than she had in a long time. She had finally met a nice guy who wasn't after her just for sex—at least not that she could tell. From the moment she'd met him, she'd had a feeling of safety and security. She didn't know why, but she felt he was a nice guy. It was hard to explain, so she tried not to worry about it. For now, she was just glad to be happy instead of scared. The past couple of days had been hard on her, but now they seemed almost like they had happened to someone else.

She went about her nightly rituals and checked the door lock just once before she got into bed. Once in bed, she lay there staring at the ceiling. Her body felt tired, but her mind was too awake for her to sleep. Instead, she just lay there thinking about Raiel. She thought it was an odd name, but wasn't sure whether or not she should ask him about it. It was probably foreign or a family name.

Lydia had given Raiel her number but hadn't gotten his. It worried her a little bit because the few times she had given men her number, she hadn't heard anything from them. She hoped that wouldn't happen with Raiel. He was too nice of a guy for her to let him get away. *Who knows? Maybe he's the one for me*, she mused.

Lydia turned onto her side and stared out the window at the building across the alley. She was worried about what to tell him about her occupation. She wanted to be honest with him, but she was scared that he would be mad about her being a stripper and not want to have anything to do with her. What if he told her she had to quit and find a different job? She wouldn't mind having a different job, but she couldn't afford everything she wanted on the low starting salaries most places paid. She didn't mind giving up stripping, but she really hated to give up the money it paid. In the end, she decided that maybe it would be best if she waited to see what happened before she told him. If it didn't work out, then she wouldn't have to say anything about it to him. Then again, if it did work out, there would be a better chance of him staying with her, even if he did get mad about her lying to him.

Lydia didn't know how long she tossed and turned, but eventually she fell asleep.

The next morning when she woke up, her excitement hadn't been quelled. She got out of bed and showered before making coffee. She ate her breakfast and drank her coffee, not really tasting either. Then she went off to her classes, not really paying any attention in any of them. After her classes, she went to work but wasn't really into it. She went out on stage and did her performances, but they were rather lackluster and her tips showed it. She didn't look anyone in the eyes or try to draw anyone to the stage. She just danced, wanting to finish and be done for the night.

After showering and getting dressed, she got a lecture from her manager. She listened to what he had to say but didn't retain much of it. She tolerated his speech until he finished, and then she left the club. Despite being scolded, she still felt better than she had in a long time. She hadn't heard from Raiel yet, but it had only been one day. Guys usually waited a day or two before calling so that they didn't come off as too desperate.

She was walking down the street, her mind wandering on its own, when she realized that she was going the wrong way. She looked around, trying to get her bearings, and then she stopped cold in her tracks. She found herself looking at a small church. She didn't remember seeing it earlier, but the feeling that she had been there before was intense. She stood, staring at the building, unable to decide what her next move should be. She wanted to go inside and check it out, but the feeling of familiarity was accompanied by one of dread. She swallowed hard, trying to work up the nerve to move up the sidewalk. Just then, a car drove by, its headlights illuminating the houses surrounding it. The sight of the houses made her wake from her stupor. She started up the sidewalk, her nerves still overactive, but not so frayed that she couldn't overcome them. She told herself she was being silly and that she shouldn't worry about it. Then she opened the church doors and went inside.

The inside of the church was rather small, but had a very homey feel. It was bright and inviting, as she imagined a church should feel. She walked in further, not seeing anyone as she went. She reached the front just as an older man came up the stairs beside the altar.

From his dress, Lydia knew he was a priest. He looked up at her with a start.

"Sorry, Father," Lydia said. "I didn't mean to startle you. I just saw the lights on and decided to come in."

"That's fine, my child. I'm just getting old, and my heart jumps easier now."

The priest carried the stack of papers he had in his hands up to the front and set them on the altar. He walked back down and sat in the first pew, indicating for Lydia to do the same. She walked over and sat next to him, leaving a little bit of room between them.

"I'm Father Stephens. What brings you out here tonight, Lydia?"

"How do you know my name?" Lydia asked. She looked down at her clothing to see if she was wearing some sort of identifying tag that she had forgotten.

"I know a lot of things, especially lately," Father Stephens started. "I call it a gift from God, but you can call it being psychic if you're more comfortable with that."

"I'd prefer not to," Lydia said. "I don't believe in that type of stuff."

"You will," Father Stephens said. "There are forces at work that you may not understand at the moment. I know that you're going to be in great danger, caught in the middle of a momentous battle between good and evil. There will be two players in this battle—an angel of the lord and one of Lucifer's fallen—and you'll have to choose which to follow."

"What are you talking about?" Lydia asked. "I came here for comfort and understanding from a man of God, but instead you start rambling like a madman."

"I'm sorry," Father Stephens said. "I know how this must sound, but what I'm telling you is true."

"I think I made a mistake coming here," Lydia said. She stood and headed for the back of the church.

"Please," Father Stephens said. "You came here for answers and that's what I gave to you."

"You gave me stories of angels and demons," Lydia said.

"Please, hear me out," Father Stephens said. "I have to warn you about the fallen angel. He will try to seduce you into joining him and he won't take no for an answer. He will speak only lies. He wants you to be with him in the coming days, and he will—"

"Stop it!" Lydia yelled. "I don't know what's wrong with you, but I'm not going to stand here and listen to your stories."

Lydia turned away and ran from the church. Father Stephens watched her go, unsure whether he had done the right thing. He didn't want to unload all this information on her at once, but time was short. He felt that this was the only way to help her. If she had been a half hour earlier she could have met Raiel. Perhaps if he had been there he could have helped explain matters to her. Lydia needed to know what was coming so that she could be prepared.

CHAPTER 18 - JETREL

Sam led Jetrel to a small restaurant in the middle of the slums. The place was run-down but appeared clean. The air was heavy with cigarette smoke, and an old radio that hung above the counter played a mournful old country song. They sat down, looked over the menu, decided what they wanted, and then went to the counter to order. The cook was the one to take their orders while a skinny older woman sat near the register reading a magazine and not looking up once.

After ordering, the two men sat back down in the old booth. The plastic seats were ripped; some were patched with duct tape, while others continued to spill cotton batting. Jetrel and Sam took turns going to the restroom to wash up and then sat in the booth making small talk until the food arrived. The food was delivered by the cook while the woman at the register continued to read about what was hot in fashion.

The food was great, and the two men ate their meals in silence. Once they had finished eating, Sam called the cook over. He came over reluctantly, grumbling under his breath.

"Jetrel, this is Phil," Sam said. "Phil, this is Jetrel. He's a new friend of mine and I thought maybe he could use your help."

"What kind of help?" Phil asked.

"Do you care if we go take a look at the goods?" Sam asked.

Phil looked Jetrel over for a moment and then shrugged. Sam got up and followed the cook to the kitchen. Jetrel decided it couldn't hurt to see what merchandise the cook was selling, so he got up and followed the two men.

The three of them walked through the kitchen and out the back door. Once outside, they walked over to a beat-up green station wagon. The cook opened up the back, pulled out a large plastic tote, and opened it up. Inside was a variety of different weapons.

There were Tasers, handguns, knives, clubs, and even some exotic stuff like throwing stars. Jetrel stepped up and started looking through the box, moving things around to get a look at the weapons at the bottom. He rooted through the box for several minutes, pulling out a small pistol that he tucked into the back of his pants. There were several other weapons he considered, but in the end, he decided that the pistol was all he should need.

Phil put the lid on the tote and pushed it into the back of the station wagon. He locked up the car, and the three men went back inside. When they got to the booth, Jetrel turned back to Phil.

"So how much do I owe you?" Jetrel asked.

"Three hundred," the cook said. He had the raspy voice of a longtime smoker, a habit Jetrel had never really understood.

"A little high, isn't it?" Jetrel asked. He didn't know how much a gun should cost, but three hundred seemed like a bit much for a small pistol. Phil shrugged and Sam started laughing. Jetrel pulled the biker's wallet out of his coat and fished out three hundred dollars. He was lucky that the biker had been carrying plenty of money, or he might have had a tougher time of things.

Phil took the money and stuck it into the front of his apron. The woman at the register was looking up at them for the first time since they had walked in. Apparently when money was involved, she developed an interest in what was going on around her. Jetrel offered his hand to Phil, who waved it away and turned to go back into the kitchen. Jetrel shook his head and turned to the woman at the counter who was once again reading her magazine.

"What do I owe you?"

"Food's free with purchase," the woman said, not looking up at them. Jetrel looked at her for a minute, debating whether or not to hit her. In the end, he decided it was probably best not to, in case he needed to come back for more weapons later. He turned and left the restaurant, Sam following close behind.

Once they were outside, Sam asked again whether Jetrel wanted to go to his place and have a few drinks. Jetrel wanted to go find someplace to shower and get some sleep, but decided he would go with Sam to whatever hole he slept in. He might need Sam's connections again, so it was probably better to stay on a friendly basis with him. Plus, Sam could probably show him how to use the pistol.

The two men walked through the nearly deserted streets, neither speaking. Jetrel was too tired for conversation, and Sam seemed anxious to get home and start drinking. Along the way, Sam removed the small whiskey bottle from his pocket and took a quick swallow before offering it to Jetrel, who debated it but refused. The last thing he needed to do was get drunk and allow the angel to get the drop on him again.

Sam led Jetrel to an old abandoned building with a small window just above the ground. Sam lay on his stomach and pushed the window open. He slid through the small opening, wriggling like a practiced contortionist. Then Jetrel followed, but he had a lot more difficulty than Sam; it took him several minutes to manipulate his body enough to squeeze through.

Once inside, Jetrel realized that they were in an abandoned clothing store. Mannequin parts were scattered all over the floor, but all the clothing was gone, probably taken by bums long ago. There were several vagrants sleeping on the floor, some with tattered blankets and others in only their layers of clothing. Sam tugged at Jetrel's sleeve and led him toward the back of the store into what had once been the stockroom. From there, they went down a staircase into the basement, Sam walking with confidence through the dark. Jetrel struggled to keep up, stumbling and slipping several times. Sam clicked on a light hanging from a wire in the middle of the room. He opened an old steel door and walked through it. Jetrel followed him inside, then waited while Sam went back to turn the light off. He told Jetrel that he didn't need it, but thought it might make him feel better. Jetrel didn't want to admit it, but it had made him feel better.

Sam took hold of Jetrel's arm and led him a little further down the tunnel before stopping and clicking on an old battery-powered lantern. The place was nothing more than a niche in the wall where some sort of machine had once stood. There was an old grungy sleeping bag, which was surrounded by all manner of trash and debris. There were a few half-full bottles of alcohol along one wall next to a couple packages of chips and beef jerky. Sam sat down amidst the debris and motioned for Jetrel to have a seat on the sleeping bag. Sam grabbed one of the bottles from along the wall; it was fuller than the others and the bottle appeared to be of a little better quality too. Sam opened the bottle of vodka and handed it to Jetrel.

"Good stuff?" Jetrel asked.

"Oh, yeah," Sam said. "It's great. I try to save it for special occasions, but have gotten into it a few times. I took it from some guy's car when he left the window halfway down. I figured if he was stupid enough to leave good alcohol in plain view, then he deserved to have it stolen. Am I right?"

Jetrel nodded his approval and took a drink. It was strong but not bad. He handed it back to Sam, who took a good drink of it and handed it back again. They passed the bottle back and forth a few times, saying very little. Jetrel took the pistol from behind his back and had Sam show him how to operate it. Sam gave him a quick rundown of how it worked and how to aim. He told Jetrel that he had learned a lot about shooting during the war. Jetrel thought about asking what war he was talking about, but then decided against it. If he got Sam talking about it, then he may be stuck there for the rest of the day listening to war stories.

Once he felt confident about using the pistol, Jetrel told Sam that he needed to get going so he could take care of some business. Sam nodded and led Jetrel back up to the street. This time, it took a lot more struggling to pull Jetrel up through the window, but they managed to get it done.

"Thanks for helping me out, Sam. I won't forget it."

"No problem. Thanks for dinner tonight."

"Hey, I owed it to you for saving my life."

"Well, if you ever want to come over and have a drink, you know where to find me."

"That I do," Jetrel said. "I'll see you around, Sam."

"Good luck," Sam said.

Jetrel turned and headed down the street toward the motel where he was staying. He'd had a rough evening and was looking forward to a nice shower and some sleep. He looked back over his shoulder and saw Sam watching him. When Sam saw him look back, he began waving furiously and nearly threw himself off balance. Jetrel waved back and smiled. He could hardly believe it, but he was going to miss the old bastard.

CHAPTER 19 - FATHER STEPHENS

Father Stephens drove quickly through the streets on his way back to the church. He had gone home to get something to eat but had felt anxious being away from the church. Lately, it was the only place he felt safe.

As he drove to the church, his mind turned back to the angel who had visited him earlier. After Raiel had finished praying, they discussed his mission and what Heaven was like. Then, in return, Father Stephens had filled Raiel in about what was happening on Earth. They had talked for several hours before Raiel had decided to return to his motel room to get some sleep. Father Stephens had still had a feeling that something was bothering him, but Raiel had said there'd been nothing wrong, so he hadn't pushed the issue. If Raiel wanted to talk, he knew where to find him.

Ever since he'd started having the visions, nearly all his time had been spent at the church. It was quiet and, with the exception of services, usually empty. He would occasionally do a confession for someone, but for the most part, he left that up to the younger priest who was still rather new to the cloth but was a good kid.

Then he'd dealt with Lydia, the woman from his dream. She'd been sweet, but she hadn't seemed to grasp the kind of danger that she would soon be in. He'd tried to stress it to her, but all he'd managed to do was scare her. He knew that he had given her a lot of information very quickly, but he'd felt that he had to push the issue quickly. He'd known that once the conversation turned to the supernatural, she would have left, so he'd dumped it all on her at once before she'd been able to go. When the time had come, he'd prayed that he would be there to help her with her decision and that the dark angel wouldn't find and corrupt her.

That was another thing that had been on his mind lately—the fallen angel. The dark one was the only one of the three in his dream whom he hadn't met, but he was probably the most dangerous. If the fallen one found out he had been aiding Raiel, he would probably kill him. He wasn't afraid to die while helping others, but he felt he would be needed throughout the entire ordeal. This whole thing was coming together like a jigsaw puzzle, with each piece falling into place one by one. If one of the pieces was missing, the puzzle couldn't be completed.

When Father Stephens reached the church, he parked quickly and went inside. He scanned the room, expecting to find the dark angel waiting for him, but he saw no one. He rushed through the church and down the stairs to the basement, which was furnished and well lit. It had been turned into a meeting room and was where the young children came for Sunday school. The church would also hold its monthly meetings down there to discuss programs and events.

Father Stephens crossed the meeting room and headed into his office, which was really nothing more than a small room with a desk, filing cabinet, and a phone. He had often debated getting a computer, but figured it wouldn't get used enough to justify the cost. The church could find better ways to use the money.

He sat down at his desk and flipped the Bible open to the page he had marked. Since the visions, he had been reading up on Revelations. Then when Raiel showed up and told him about the key of the Abyss, he decided to do some research on it. He had been to the library and copied all the information he could find about it, but most of it didn't really say anything more than the Bible did.

It said that during the time before the second coming of Jesus Christ, an angel would come from Heaven, and the key of the Abyss would be given to him by the archangel Michael. With this key, the angel would open the pit and release a horde of locusts with the ability to poison their prey as a scorpion does. They were commanded not to feast on the many plants or crops, but to hurt those men who did not have the symbol of God upon their foreheads. They would not kill these men but would cause them torment for a period of five months.

Father Stephens was trying to figure out why the key should be of such importance now. If the Abyss were opened, then the worst thing that would happen is that all the sinners in the world would be tormented for five months. Without the angels to blow the horns to signal the other two woes of humanity, nothing more would happen. Death would only be brought on by the next two woes. Lucifer's minions loved tormenting mortals, but why go to such great lengths to keep the key out of the angel's hands?

Plus the key of the Abyss only came into play near the end of Revelations. There had been none of the other signs or signals that should have preceded the end of days.

Father Stephens sat in his office rereading all the information he had gathered, but he was no closer to figuring out what was going on than he had been the first time he'd read it. The more he read, the more certain he was that he was missing something, which caused him to read it all again. He was being pulled deeper into his obsession but felt helpless to stop it. He had to do whatever he could to figure out why all this was happening and where he could find the key.

Father Stephens forced himself to set the Bible down and put his paperwork aside. He rubbed his eyes and stretched before getting up and going upstairs. He walked through the empty, quiet church and went out the front doors. He stood outside on the sidewalk and looked up at the night sky. The night was cool, and the skies were clear and seemingly bursting with stars. He watched the stars for several minutes, ignoring the cold that was causing him to shiver. Something major was about to happen and he had no idea what it was. He would have felt better if he knew what to expect, but he knew nothing. He kept waiting for God to give him another vision that would clarify things, but that vision never came. He was a man of great patience, but his patience was waning.

Father Stephens turned around and walked back into the church. He had hoped that a few minutes outside would have helped to ease his mind, but it had done little to alleviate his fears. He knew that if he wanted to clear his mind, he needed to spend more than a few minutes away from the church and at a greater distance than ten feet. He just felt like this was where he needed to be in case something happened. If he hadn't been there in the middle of the night, he wouldn't have met Raiel or Lydia. He felt that this was a good indication that he needed to remain there as long as necessary.

He was returning to his office and had nearly reached the basement stairs, when he heard the front doors open. He turned, expecting to see Raiel. He knew that the angel had many questions and knew that he would be back to try to find the answers. What he saw instead nearly stopped his heart in his chest. The figure standing across the room from him wasn't anyone he had seen before, but was one he had been expecting. Father Stephens said a prayer silently to himself, for across from him was none other than the fallen one.

CHAPTER 20 - RAIEL

Raiel had ditched his police uniform and was now dressed in a white polo shirt, jeans, and a nice pair of brown leather dress shoes. He felt like he fit in much better, and he would be well dressed for his date with Lydia that night. He had waited almost a day to call her, but couldn't stand to let it go on any longer, so he had called from the little diner where they'd had coffee on the night they'd met. He was a little bit worried that he was having such strong feelings for her. He had been warned about associating romantically with humans. They were from two different worlds and those worlds didn't mesh. It could never work out.

Raiel didn't care what the elder angels had told him. He just wanted to get to know Lydia better. Besides, he was already on the outs with God, so it didn't matter. If he could manage to get the key of the Abyss and deliver it to God, then he was sure all would be forgiven. After all, he wasn't the first angel to be seduced by the darker side of Earth, and they'd all been forgiven and allowed to return to Heaven. So all he had to do was find the key, but that could wait until later. The fallen one was out of the way, so he could find the key at his leisure. Eventually, Hell would send another dark angel to search for the key, but it would take some time. It took Heaven a long time to prepare him for his mission to Earth, so he was sure it would be the same in Hell. Then once he got here, it would take a few days to fully recover, which would be more than enough time to find the key. He planned on starting his search the next day. That night, though, he had a date, which had been the only thing on his mind all day.

Raiel decided to go to the church to visit with Father Stephens before his date with Lydia. He had more questions for him and had even been debating telling him what happened during his prayers the other night.

When he reached the church and went inside, he found Father Stephens sitting on the steps in front of the altar with his head in his hands. Raiel stood for a moment, wondering what had happened. He looked around the church but didn't see anyone or anything out of place. Then he ran up to the priest and knelt in front of him.

"What's wrong, Father? Did something happen?"

Father Stephens shook his head and remained as he was. Raiel sat, waiting for some sort of explanation. He was about to ask again, when Father Stephens lifted his head. He looked at Raiel, who could see that he had been crying. There were no tears now, but his face was red and puffy. He opened his mouth as if to say something, but closed it again. He swallowed hard and then started again.

"I had a visitor last night."

"Who was it, Father?"

"The fallen one—Jetrel."

Raiel's hands clenched into fists, and he restrained the urge to grab Father Stephens and shout for him to speak faster. He thought he had killed the dark angel, but apparently the fallen one was more resourceful than he had first thought. He swore to himself that he wouldn't make the same mistake twice. The next time he encountered the fallen one—or Jetrel, as Father Stephens called him—he would make sure he was dead. He knew that he couldn't kill the fallen one, but he could destroy the body and send him back to Hell.

"He came into the church in the middle of the night, as you did," Father Stephens said. "He had many questions for me but never made any sort of threatening gestures toward me. I tried to cast him out, but he wouldn't leave. He kept asking questions, some that made me start to doubt myself and my feelings toward others. I actually started to doubt my own faith and the commitment to my calling as a priest. His visit was disturbing and enlightening at the same time."

"The fallen ones have very sharp tongues, and they are experts at using them to cut you where you're most vulnerable," Raiel said. "You are an excellent priest and a very caring human being. If you have any faults, it's that you trust too much and are too easily taken in by the smooth words of this demon."

"I don't think he was trying to trick me. I truly believe he was sincere in his questions and his motives. But he has gone in search of the key, and I fear that no matter what his intentions are, the key will not be safe in his hands."

"Don't worry, Father. I'll go in search of Jetrel and keep him from finding the key, even if I have to destroy him to do it."

"My son," Father Stephens started, but it didn't matter. Raiel had already stood and was headed toward the church doors. Father Stephens watched him go, worried about what he would do once he found Jetrel. Even angels weren't immune to sin, and he feared that Raiel might let his emotions get the better of him. It didn't matter anymore, though; Raiel's actions were his own and out of the priest's hands. All he could do now was pray for him, and that was the one thing he was good at.

After leaving the church, Raiel stood on the sidewalk, trying to sense which way he should go. His emotions were so churned up that he wasn't able to sense anything at all from the key. In frustration, he sat down on the sidewalk and closed his eyes to meditate. He needed to gain control of his emotions and push them away so he could sense the key's location. It was there that he would find Jetrel and complete his mission.

Raiel sat on the concrete, ignoring the cold wind and the cars that occasionally drove by. He focused everything on removing the emotions from his mind and trying to sense the key. It was an artifact of immense power, containing an enormous amount of Goldenlight energy. He tried to sense the energy but was having trouble doing so.

He was nearly ready to give up and begin searching randomly, hoping that God would lead him on the path he needed to take, when he remembered Lydia and the date they were supposed to go on later that night. In his rage, he had nearly forgotten about it. He was supposed to meet her at six, which was several hours away, but if he had gotten involved with his search for the key and forgotten about the date, he would never have forgiven himself. Then he realized that the more he thought about Lydia, the quicker the anger left him.

Raiel changed his train of thought and started thinking about Lydia. He remembered their first meeting, when she had nearly run him down. Then he thought about sitting across from her while having coffee and talking at the small café. After that, he had walked her home, and they'd been able to talk even more. It hadn't mattered what they'd talked about; he'd just enjoyed hearing the sound of her voice. Then at the door, neither of them had seemed ready to end the evening. They'd stood on the front steps of her apartment building and continued talking. Finally, she'd said that it was getting late and she'd given him her phone number. He'd taken it eagerly and told her goodnight. He'd wanted to kiss her, but had thought that it was probably too soon. He'd hoped that she'd wanted to kiss him too and that she would instigate it, but she hadn't. Instead she'd smiled at him and gone into the building. Once the door had been closed, he'd stood there for several minutes before turning around and walking down the sidewalk to go find himself a motel room with his newfound money.

Raiel opened his eyes and realized that he was smiling. His rage was gone and was replaced with happiness. Amidst the happy feelings was another feeling he recognized from the descriptions he had been given in Heaven. It was a gentle pull in the front of his mind, like the magnetic needle of a compass being pulled toward true north. He stood up and followed the pull, hoping he wouldn't be too late to stop Jetrel.

CHAPTER 21 - JETREL

After Jetrel left Sam, he was filled with a mixture of emotions. He was glad that he had met him and that they had gotten to spend time together. But he was also sad that it had to end so soon, and he wondered if he would see him again before going back to Hell. Thinking about Hell upset him as well. He was starting to realize that he didn't want to give up everything he had experienced on Earth. It was something they had warned him about in Hell, but only in passing. They'd been more concerned about demons becoming obsessed with the seemingly unlimited amount of sinning that could be found on Earth. He assumed that it was because they hadn't been worried about him becoming attached to people and enjoying a life without torment. It definitely hadn't been something he had ever considered.

Jetrel had planned on going back to his motel room to clean up and wash his clothes before going to bed, but now he didn't feel like it. He needed to walk and clear his head. There was so much going on with his emotions that he almost felt like giving up and staying on Earth. Even if he decided to do that, he knew it wouldn't last. Once the angels had the key, other fallen ones would be sent to bring him back to Hell. Then he would be tortured for an eternity for failing the master, and he would be even worse off than he already was. On the other hand, if he did get the key, he would be dooming humanity to an eternity of torment and horrors. Either way, he would be miserable.

Jetrel didn't know how long he had been walking, but when he looked up, he was in an unfamiliar part of the city. He looked around, trying to get his bearings, when he spotted a small church in the distance. Something about that church seemed to call out to him, and he found that he had no choice but to walk toward it.

Jetrel's feet led him right up to the large oak double doors. It was late, but the lights were on. He took hold of the doorknob, opened the door, and stepped into the small church. He barely had time to register the surroundings before something else caught his eye. A priest stood at the front of the church, staring at him in obvious surprise. Jetrel and the priest looked at each other for a few moments before the priest finally managed to speak.

"I know who you are, evil one, and I don't want your kind in my church."

"You're banishing me?" Jetrel asked.

"I would do much worse to you if I had the strength. I know of your goals and I will do whatever I can to stop you. This is a holy place, and a creature of darkness dare not trespass here. Now in the name of the Father, the Son, and the Holy Ghost, I banish you from this dwelling." The priest stepped forward, producing a bottle of holy water from his pocket and pulling the cork with his teeth. He flung the contents at Jetrel, who stepped aside and brought his arm up to protect his face. A little splashed onto his hand and started burning. Jetrel wiped the water on his jeans, spit on the wound, and wiped it off on his pants again. The burning had stopped, but there was still a sore spot.

"Do you make a habit of carrying holy water with you?" Jetrel asked.

"I've been waiting for you to seek me out, and I wanted to be prepared. What do you want from me, demon?"

"My name's Jetrel and I came here to seek your help."

"I will offer no aid to one of the fallen. Now leave my church before I cast you out physically." The priest stepped forward bravely, but Jetrel could plainly see him breathing heavily and sweating profusely. He put on a good front, but it was a bluff and they both knew it. The priest could no more throw him out with force than Jetrel could lift a car over his head.

"Fine," Jetrel said. "I'll leave, but I thought that this was a place of worship, and a place to go when feeling lost. Apparently I was mistaken. This must be a place where only saints can come to seek counsel when in crisis...where you only minister to those you deem worthy. I come in peace to seek your counsel and you curse me, throw holy water at me, and banish me from the Lord's church. You claim me to be the monster, but you threaten me and tell me to leave when I've not spoken so much as an unkind word to you. I guess I'll just have to take my problems to one without such a hypocritical attitude about their vocation."

Jetrel turned to leave, while the priest stood and stared at him in shocked amazement. Jetrel pushed open the door and started down the sidewalk, when he heard the door open behind him.

"Wait!" the priest said. "Come back in and let us speak of whatever you wish. I was rude and have forgotten why I became a priest. I joined the priesthood to help those on a dark path find their way back to the light, and no matter how far down the path they are, I shouldn't turn my back on them. I'm asking you to please forgive me and for you to come back in so that we can start over on better terms."

Jetrel turned back to the priest and watched him for a moment before walking back up the path to the church's door. The priest stepped aside and held the door open for him.

"You were truly blessed with a silver tongue, Father," Jetrel said, as he entered the church. "I believe you could talk Satan himself into a life of purity."

"You give me entirely too much credit, Jetrel. I just realized how unfair I was being to you and wanted to offer you my sincerest apologies."

"Well, thank you, Father."

"It's Father Stephens, if you please."

"Thank you, Father Stephens."

"I'm just shocked to see you here. What is it you've come to ask me?"

Jetrel walked to the front of the church, sat down on the red carpeted steps, and looked at the floor. He reached down, picked up a white feather, and examined it.

"I see that the angel has been here to visit you too," Jetrel said. "What miracle did he work for you?"

"He cured me of the migraines caused by my visions."

"I can understand that. Many of the great seers were plagued by the same malady. It goes with the territory, I'm afraid."

"Is this what you've come to discuss with me, or were there deeper things on your mind?"

"You still seem nervous, Father. Are you that anxious to get rid of me? I can't say I blame you. After all, I am a demon. We've never been known as the most trustworthy of creatures."

"In my visions, I have seen one of great purity and one filled with darkness. I have met the angel Raiel and have known him to be a pure spirit."

"Then that would make me the one who's filled with great darkness, wouldn't it?"

"I can only assume as much."

"It's obvious from the formality of your speech that you're uncomfortable around me, but that's okay because I'm not entirely myself around you either."

"Well, perhaps it would be best that we get on with our parley then?"

Jetrel smiled. They had become two dueling politicians, each trying to outdo the other with his words. Neither one trusted the other nor his motives. They were each trying to find a chink in the opponent's armor.

Jetrel let the feather drop to the floor and sighed. He began his story with his days in Hell and how he tormented the souls of the damned. Then he told Father Stephens about arriving on Earth and everything he had done during his time here. It was a painful story for Jetrel, but he felt that he did an adequate job of telling it.

When he finished his story, he told Father Stephens about the feelings he had been having—first for the woman he had inadvertently rescued, to his friendship with Sam, and the sadness he felt when he thought that he might not see him again.

Father Stephens listened to the whole story in silence, not interrupting once. This was a small kindness that Jetrel appreciated. If he had stopped to discuss one of the issues, he might not have had the nerve to continue with the story. He found this whole discussion disturbing and unnatural. If he had shown any sort of emotion or weakness in Hell, he would have been ripped limb from limb and tossed into the lake of fire to burn forever.

Father Stephens had taken a seat in the front pew and was in deep thought as Jetrel finished his story. He stared at the feather on the floor, not really seeing it. Jetrel was anxious to hear what he had to say, but didn't want to push him for fear that he would lose his train of thought.

"I would imagine that your feelings are pretty natural for someone in your situation," Father Stephens said. "After all, you have spent so many years in an environment of horrible evil, that when you are finally in an environment with so many different emotions, you're bound to be overwhelmed. I don't think a soul is supposed to be so limited in the types of feelings and emotions it can experience."

"What am I supposed to do about it?"

"I don't know," Father Stephens said. "I wish I had an answer for you, but I don't. This sort of thing is outside of my realm of experience. I don't think there are going to be any easy answers for you. In the end, you're just going to have to decide what it is you want to do."

"That's just it, though. No matter what I do, I'm going to end up in the same place. I don't think I can go back there now. I've seen and felt too much. I can't go back to that kind of existence."

"Unfortunately, that's not for us to decide. All we can do is the best that we can, and help those that we can along the way."

"You don't truly think I've changed, do you? I can tell from your mannerisms."

"I wish I did, but from what I've seen in my visions, I don't believe you will change in the end."

"So you're saying that I can't change, despite my intention? Well, that's wonderful to hear."

"You asked me a question and I answered it honestly. I'm sorry if it's not the one you wanted to hear, but it's what I feel."

"You're supposed to be a man of God and love all his children. Believe it or not, I am one of his children and so is Lucifer. God loves us all, even those who have strayed from their path. If I can't depend upon a priest to try to lead me on my path, then I might as well give up now."

"Please don't be that way. I have heard your tale and offered you the most help I can. There's nothing I can do to change the paths that others have taken and, unfortunately, you have taken a dark path—one that I'm afraid you won't be able to turn from."

"Thank you for taking the time to listen to me, even if it was with a closed mind. I don't know what you've seen in your visions, but I choose my own actions. Now if you don't mind, I have a key to find."

Jetrel stood up and stormed out of the church, despite Father Stephens' calls for him to stop. He had heard all he needed to, and now he knew that everyone had already written him off as a lost cause. If that was the case, then the only thing left to do was find the key and return it to Hell. At least there he knew exactly what others thought of him and where he stood with them.

Father Stephens watched the door close behind Jetrel but didn't chase after him. He knew it wouldn't do any good. He hadn't heeded any of his calls to stop and wouldn't do so outside either. He knew he had failed horribly with Jetrel and was beginning to feel badly about it. He had let his anger and fear of the fallen angel cloud his judgment. All he had done was make the situation worse. Now Jetrel was upset and angry with only one thing on his mind.

Father Stephens turned and walked to the steps where Jetrel had been sitting. He sat down, buried his face in his hands, and began to weep. He had failed with Jetrel and now, because of him, there was another soul out there in pain. He was supposed to help those in need, no matter who they were. Jetrel's words had cut him deeply, and all he could do was wait to see what kind of evil he had just unleashed upon the world.

CHAPTER 22 - RAIEL

Raiel followed the compass in his mind into the slums of the city. He didn't know how much of a lead Jetrel had, so he tried to keep moving as quickly as he could. All the buildings in the neighborhood were horribly run-down and dilapidated. He walked amidst them, trying to determine where he was being led. He finally managed to narrow it down to an old clothing store. He circled the building several times, trying to find a way in. He tried the doors as nonchalantly as he could, but they were locked, as were all the windows within reach. He walked to the alley and considered trying to use the fire escape to get to the roof, when he noticed a small window at ground level. He knelt down and pushed it open easily. He got down on the ground, trying not to dirty up his white shirt, and wriggled through it.

The inside of the old building was lit rather well, due to the large number of windows. Raiel saw that scattered across the floor were a large number of mannequin parts amidst the newspapers and filth. The whole building smelled of feces and urine. He looked around the room but saw no sign of the vagrants who had apparently made the building their home. He walked around the old building, eventually finding a set of stairs leading to the basement. He tried the light switch, but nothing happened. He didn't figure it would work, but it was worth a try. There probably hadn't been electricity in the building in years.

Raiel walked back through the building, eventually finding a partially burned candle. He took the lighter from his pocket and headed back to the stairway, lighting the candle as he went. It wasn't exactly the light source he had hoped for, but it was better than nothing. Raiel headed down the stairs slowly, holding one hand in front of the candle to keep it from blowing out as he walked. If this was going to be the pace he'd have to move at the whole way, then he would never catch up to Jetrel.

Raiel got to the bottom of the stairs and found himself in a small room with a single lightbulb hanging from a wire. He pulled on the chain and was surprised when the light clicked on. He looked at the wire, which was spliced in the middle to an old extension cord that ran along one of the rafters before it disappeared through the ceiling. Someone had evidently rigged this light up to run off the power that ran into one of the other buildings on this block. He didn't think the splicing job looked too safe, but it did the job it was intended for.

Raiel walked to the door on the other side of the room and opened it slowly. Light spilled into the narrow hallway, illuminating the assorted trash lining the floor. He started down the hallway, continuing to guard the flame of the candle with his hand. Partway down the hall, he saw a little niche in the wall where a vagrant had apparently been staying for quite a while. The old sleeping bag had been worn almost threadbare, and there were old newspapers in a pile, the oldest from over a year ago. There were alcohol bottles lining the wall. Most of them were empty, but the ones nearest the head of the sleeping bag were still partially full. He was about to turn away when something caught his eye. Partially buried under a pile of trash was a small battery-powered lantern. He picked it up and checked it over before turning it on. The bulbs blazed to life, and Raiel blew out his candle and set it on the ground where the lantern had been.

Raiel took his new lantern and continued following the narrow hallway. There were several points where it branched off, but he was always able to use his mental compass to determine which way he was supposed to go. He didn't know how long or how far he had been traveling when he first heard the digging noises, but it had been a long ways. He turned his lantern off and tried to gauge where the sounds were coming from. He put his hand on the wall and followed it toward the sound of the digging. He stumbled a few times as he went. A couple of times, he had to stop and use the lighter to gain his bearings. He didn't dare light the lantern in case whoever was digging—he assumed it was Jetrel, but couldn't be completely sure—would see the light and know he was there.

Eventually, he started to see a light in the distance and was able to follow it to its source. When Raiel was close enough to see what was going on, but far enough away to keep from being seen, he stopped and surveyed the scene.

There were two men standing around a small hole in the ground. One of them had a shovel and the other one was holding up a lantern much like the one Raiel had found. The man holding the light was dressed in ratty clothing and had a bushy, unkempt beard. Raiel assumed that this man was a vagrant, but had no idea why he would be working with Jetrel. Surely Jetrel had told him some sort of outrageous lie to get him to help and would probably kill the bum when he was done using him.

The second man, the one wielding the shovel, was a young man with black hair. He was dressed in a tattered old Sturgis shirt and a pair of jeans filled with holes and worn patches. He was definitely the fallen one he had thrown in the dumpster before. He even noticed he still wore his boots without the laces and that the tongues flopped forward almost comically.

Jetrel wiped the sweat from his forehead before he knelt back down and continued to pry stones from the floor to add to the small pile next to him. Raiel felt the compass in his head directing him toward the ground where they were digging. Jetrel had found the location of the key first, but had been slowed down by the process of having to dig out the old stones that lined the floor of the tunnel. Raiel was lucky that the key hadn't been easier to get to. If it had been, then Jetrel would have gotten to it first, Raiel's mission would have failed, and then all humanity would have to suffer for his failure.

Raiel knew that he had to stop Jetrel before he managed to unearth the key, but the addition of a second person had him worried. He believed him to be nothing more than a common vagrant, but that didn't mean he wasn't dangerous. Now Raiel wished he had thought ahead and brought the gun he had taken from the cop, so he could have simply shot them both and taken the key.

Raiel turned away from the two men and quietly made his way back toward the entrance. Once he was far enough away, he turned the lantern back on and made his way back to the store's old sales floor, where he began searching for some sort of weapon. He wanted to go get his gun, but he didn't know how much time he had. He was already feeling anxious being gone this long, but he needed something to help even out the odds. He started kicking through the debris on the floor, concentrating on the areas near where he had found the candle and lighter. He felt his foot hit something solid and it rolled across the floor away from him. He walked over and picked up a baseball bat that had been hidden beneath one of the sleeping bags scattered throughout the old showroom floor. He held it firmly and took a few practice swings before smiling and heading back to the tunnels.

Raiel made good time on his way back through the tunnels, having already traversed them once. He made it back to where he had first heard the sounds of digging, turned his lantern off, and crept quietly back to his position just out of sight of the two men. He saw that a few more rocks had been added to the pile, but the two men had apparently decided to take a break. They each sat, leaning against one of the walls.

The vagrant took a drink from a small bottle and then handed it to Jetrel, who took a drink and handed it back. Raiel wondered how much they had been drinking and for how long. If they were drunk, it would make this whole encounter a lot easier.

The two sat against the wall for a few minutes, but Jetrel didn't take another drink. Raiel was a little disappointed, but felt a little better when he saw the other man taking several more. A few minutes passed before Jetrel got up and started digging again. Raiel waited until they were concentrating on their digging before slipping out of the shadows and into the lantern's light. He moved up to them quietly, getting right next to them before they realized he was there.

Jetrel started to shout a warning to the man with the lantern, but Raiel clubbed him across the back of the neck. The man dropped the lantern and collapsed to the ground. The lantern rolled into the hole they had been digging, but didn't break. It caused large shadows to jump onto the walls, creating an eerie effect. Jetrel ran at Raiel and punched him across the jaw. Raiel stumbled back and Jetrel pushed his attack. Raiel regained his footing and drove the end of the bat into Jetrel's ribs. Jetrel stopped short and fell to his knees, clutching his ribs. Raiel leapt at him, knocking him onto his back. The two of them wrestled on the stone floor, each one throwing punches. Raiel drove his elbow into Jetrel's ribs where he had hit them with the bat, and Jetrel screamed. Raiel rolled on top of him and pinned his arms with his legs. Raiel grabbed the shovel that Jetrel had dropped and lifted it above his head with the blade pointing down. It might take several tries, but he figured he could use it to decapitate Jetrel. Then he would use that same shovel to unearth the key of the Abyss.

Raiel yelled as someone clubbed him across the back. He dropped the shovel and turned to see the bum swinging the bat at him again. This one hit Raiel across the side of the head, sending a shower of sparks cascading before his eyes. He lunged at the man, while trying to remain conscious. The man with the bat stumbled and Raiel ran past him. He struggled to reach his lantern and barely managed to grab it while remaining upright. He weaved his way back down the tunnels, fighting the urge to vomit. He had to get away from there before he passed out. He was in no condition to fight and had a feeling that Jetrel was hurt pretty badly as well. He would probably need to be taken to a hospital, which would buy Raiel some time to come back for the key. The only thing he was concerned about now was making his way out of the tunnels in case Jetrel and the homeless guy came after him. If they found him lying unconscious on the tunnel floor, he would be killed. He wished he had just killed Jetrel outright when he'd had the chance, but he couldn't do anything about it now. All he knew was that Jetrel would die by his hands; he would make him suffer for what he had done to Father Stephens and for what he had just done to him. Both Jetrel and the homeless guy would pay dearly.

CHAPTER 23 - JETREL

Jetrel left the church in a rage. He had gone there for answers and help, but had found only suspicion and blame. What he'd wanted was to be able to have a civilized conversation with Father Stephens, but the old man had only pointed fingers. None of it mattered now, though. If he was going to be labeled evil, then he may as well earn that label. The best way for him to do that would be to find the key of the Abyss and return it to Hell.

Jetrel made his way toward his motel room, intending to clean himself up before going out to search for the key. When he got there, he took off his clothes and showered. He was going to get dressed and go out again, but he decided that he would wash his clothes and get some sleep before starting on his mission. He wasn't in any condition to try to locate the key. His mind would need to be clear to be able to sense its location.

Jetrel washed his clothes in the bathtub, using shampoo. He rinsed them and hung them to dry before wiping his jacket down and hanging it to dry as well. He kept meaning to try to find new clothing, but something always managed to distract him—not that it would matter too much anyway, since he would more than likely find the key the next day and return to Hell with it.

Once Jetrel finished cleaning up, he crawled into bed to get some sleep. The next day would be busy, and he could use the rest before tackling his objective.

When Jetrel awoke the next morning, his rage had subsided. He was still mad, but not nearly to the extent he had been the day before. He got up and dressed before heading out of the motel room. He stopped by a small corner store to buy something to eat and had a quick breakfast of powdered donuts and pop on the walk back to the room.

Once at the motel, Jetrel lay down on the bed, closed his eyes, and began to focus on the key. He lay there meditating on the key for several hours before the little compass in his mind started to turn toward its destination. Jetrel opened his eyes and got up, the feeling of the key still strong within him. He left his motel room again and started walking in the direction that he was being pulled.

Jetrel was led through the city and back into the familiar areas of the slums. He walked through them, trying to get a better focus on where he was being led. He ended up outside the old clothing store where Sam lived. He thought about just going inside, but remembered how dark the tunnels had been and decided instead to stop at a pawnshop he had seen on the way there and pick up some supplies.

Jetrel went into the shop and found a battery-powered lantern similar to the one Sam had used in the tunnels. Then he searched for other tools he might need, but the only other thing he thought would be useful was a shovel. So he bought those two items and headed back to the old clothing store.

Once he got to the old store, he went into the alley and wriggled his way inside through the small window near the alley floor. He looked around and saw that the bums who had been there before were gone. They were probably outside searching for food or hitting people up for money. He turned on the lantern and crossed through the old stockroom before heading down the stairs. He saw the old light hanging from the ceiling that Sam had turned on to help him get his bearings. But Jetrel didn't turn it on; he had his lantern and didn't need anything else. He opened the old steel door that led to the steam tunnels and went inside.

"Sam?" Jetrel asked once he was inside the tunnel.

"What?" Sam asked. "Who's there?"

"It's Jetrel. Do you remember me from the other night?"

"Oh, yeah I remember you. You're the guy I pulled out of the dumpster."

Jetrel smiled at that and walked back to Sam's niche in the wall. Sam was struggling to sit up, and Jetrel waited until he had succeeded before sitting down himself on an old cinderblock that looked relatively clean.

"What are you doing here?" Sam asked.

"I'm not sure," Jetrel said, "but I think I could use your help."

"Help with what?"

Jetrel sighed and began to fill Sam in on who he was and what he was doing. He left out the part about him being a fallen angel and only referred to himself as an angel. With the exception of a few indiscretions that might not have shown him in a favorable light, he told Sam everything. It took a while, but Sam waited patiently for Jetrel to finish his story. When he was done, Sam said about the only thing a person could say after hearing a story like that—"I think you're full of shit."

"I promise you I'm not," Jetrel told him, "but it doesn't matter if you believe me or not. All I really want to know is if you'll help me."

"Sure, why not. I've got nothing better to do today."

Jetrel helped Sam to his feet, and the two headed further into the steam tunnels. Jetrel was in the lead, using the pull of the key to guide him. They walked for quite a while before Jetrel stopped. He felt the pull of the key directly beneath him somewhere under the stone floor. He handed the lantern to Sam and had him hold it up over the area. Jetrel used the shovel and started trying to pry the old rocks from the floor. It was slow work, but once he managed to get the first rock out, it was much easier to pry the rest loose.

Jetrel took his jacket off and pulled the gun out of the waist of his jeans. He set the gun on the ground and put his jacket on top of it in case anyone happened to show up unexpectedly. He doubted anyone else would venture down into these musty old tunnels, but he had learned to always be ready for anything. He then started prying rocks out of the floor again.

The old tunnels were very warm, and Jetrel began to sweat as he worked to break the stones loose from the old mortar. He wiped the sweat from his face and sighed. This was much tougher than he had hoped it would be. He set back to work, prying stones loose and tossing them onto the ever-growing pile next to him. He had been working for only ten minutes when his back started to tighten up, so he decided to take a little break.

The two men sat down, leaning heavily against one of the walls. They talked a little about Jetrel's mission, but nothing too serious. Jetrel didn't think that Sam believed him, but he figured was still willing to go along with it for no other reason than that it was something to do. Sam reached into his coat pocket, pulled out the bottle of whiskey, and took a drink of it before offering it to Jetrel. Jetrel took a drink from the bottle. The whiskey was warm all the way down, but it was a good warmth. He handed the bottle back to Sam, who took a drink and offered it back again. Jetrel considered it, but waved it away. He didn't need to be getting drunk while he was searching for the key. He didn't know what to expect when he found it, but he might need to think quickly if the situation called for it. Sam didn't seem to mind, though. He simply took the bottle back and had another drink.

The two men sat in silence for several minutes, until Jetrel felt like his back had relaxed enough to allow him to continue digging. He went back to the hole and started trying to pry the stones loose again while Sam resumed his position as holder of the light.

Jetrel was so focused on his work that he didn't even notice that someone was sneaking up on them until it was too late. He looked up and tried to shout a warning to Sam, but the guy cracked Sam across the back of the neck with a baseball bat. The lantern fell from Sam's hand and rolled into the hole, while Sam collapsed in a heap on the floor.

Jetrel noticed that familiar buzz in the back of his mind, which indicated this was Raiel. Jetrel charged him and punched him in the face. Raiel stumbled back and Jetrel moved to attack again, but Raiel stopped himself and slammed the top of the bat into Jetrel's ribs. Jetrel felt an intense pain as he heard his ribs crack. He clutched his right side, unable to breath. He fell to his knees and Raiel leapt on him, knocking him onto his back. The two angels began fighting to gain an advantage, each throwing punches when he had the opportunity. Finally, Raiel drove his elbow into Jetrel's ribs, causing Jetrel to scream. Raiel used the opportunity to roll on top of him and pin his arms to his sides. Jetrel tried to fight back, but couldn't do anything because of the pain in his ribs, which was further increased by Raiel sitting on his chest. Raiel grabbed the shovel and held it up with the blade pointing down. Jetrel tried to find some way of moving before Raiel could drive the head of the shovel through his throat, but with Raiel's weight crushing the wind from his lungs, he couldn't even find the strength to scream.

Suddenly, Sam stepped up behind Raiel and swung the discarded bat, striking him across the back. Raiel screamed and rolled off Jetrel, allowing him to take a painful breath. Jetrel curled up into a ball, clutching his ribs. He tried to open his eyes to witness the end of the fight, but he passed out from the pain.

CHAPTER 24 - LYDIA

Lydia had been sitting in her apartment for over an hour, waiting on Raiel to show up. She had been excited about her date with him, but that excitement had now turned to frustration. She had thought he was a nice guy and couldn't believe that he would stand her up. Besides, he was a cop, and cops were supposed to be trustworthy and dependable.

She really felt like she needed a night out, especially after the week she'd been having. First, it was the attempted rape and murder, and then the stalker who had resulted in her meeting Raiel in the first place. Then it was her surreal encounter with Father Stephens, and now she was getting flak from Mike at work about her job performance. He'd told her that she had seemed distracted, that she hadn't seemed into it anymore. He'd said that some of the customers had been complaining—especially her regulars. They'd come in expecting special treatment from her, but had felt that she had been ignoring them. Then he'd said that if she didn't start showing more enthusiasm on the dance floor, he would replace her with another dancer, and he'd assured her that there were many other girls looking for positions in his club.

Lydia had promised him that she would try harder to turn things around. He'd then kicked her out of his office. Now she was left wondering how she would be able to turn things around when she had lost all desire to dance. Her mind was so preoccupied with everything going on in her life that she didn't have anything left to devote to her job.

Now, the one thing she had been looking forward to didn't look like it was going to happen. She looked at the clock again and sighed. If she'd had a phone number where she could reach him, she would have tried. All she could do, though, was sit on her couch, feeling helpless and rejected.

She had just about talked herself into going out without him when she heard a knock on her apartment door. She went to the door and opened it, gasping when she saw Raiel leaning against the doorframe. He was beaten and bloody, his clothes were a mess, and he looked like he was dangerously close to passing out. He tried stepping into her apartment, but stumbled and she caught him. She put her arm around him, helped him into her living room, and sat him down on her couch.

"What happened?" Lydia asked.

"I got mugged," Raiel said. He had debated telling her the truth, but then decided against it. The less she really knew about him and what he was doing on Earth, the better it would be. Plus getting mugged was a believable story. People got mugged and beaten every day.

"Oh my God," Lydia said. "I think we should take you to the hospital."

"No," Raiel said quickly. He had considered going to the hospital himself, but he would have been caught for sure. By now, there were probably pictures and descriptions of him being distributed to every hospital in the city, not to mention the fact that he still had no identification, and that would bring the cops around again to question him. Even if no one at the hospital recognized him, the cops were sure to; after all, he had assaulted an officer and stolen his uniform. He had a feeling that wasn't something the cops were willing to overlook.

"Are you sure?" Lydia asked. She was a little surprised by the speed with which he had answered her. In most circumstances, someone who had been beaten this badly would have gone directly to the hospital instead of their date's house. She started to wonder if there was a reason for him not wanting to go to the hospital, or if she was just making something out of nothing. Oftentimes, she let her imagination run away with her, but something about this felt different. She had trusted him fully only a few minutes before, but with one word, she'd started to doubt everything about him.

"I just don't like hospitals," Raiel said, as if reading her mind. "I had a bad experience in a hospital once, and I've been terrified of them ever since."

Raiel smiled at Lydia, hoping it would ease the troubled look that he saw on her face. Lydia returned the smile, her suspicions not entirely eased by his excuse. There was something in that smile she didn't trust. That combined with his reaction to her hospital suggestion put her on her guard. She would try to act normally around him but would remain cautious. More than likely this was just a case of her imagination running wild, but it couldn't hurt to be watchful.

Lydia went into the kitchen, got a pan of warm water and some dish towels, and carried them out to Raiel. She wet the rags and started helping him to clean his wounds. There were many bruises and very few cuts, but the ones he did have were pretty deep. Raiel took up one of the dishcloths and started to help her clean the wounds. Once they had been cleaned, she treated them with hydrogen peroxide before bandaging them up.

When Lydia and Raiel finished cleaning and bandaging his wounds, he asked if it would be alright if he went and lay down on her bed for a little bit until his head stopped pounding. Lydia helped him to her bedroom and then went to the kitchen to get some aspirin. She returned with the aspirin and a glass of water to find him sitting on the edge of her bed completely naked. She gasped and nearly dropped the glass of water as she turned away. She set the glass and aspirin on her dresser.

"I got you some aspirin and some water. I'll just leave them on the dresser for you and give you a little privacy."

"You don't have to go," Raiel said, as Lydia headed for the door. "I'm sure it's nothing you haven't seen before. I just didn't want to get your bed covered in the dirt and blood from my clothing."

Lydia stopped, although she wasn't sure why. She turned, picked up the water and aspirin, and took them to Raiel, trying to keep her eyes on his face. He took the aspirin, tossed them into his mouth, downed the whole glass of water, and handed the empty glass back to Lydia. Lydia took it and turned back toward the door, anxious to be out of there.

Raiel turned and lay back on the bed, letting out a yelp as his head bumped the headboard. Lydia turned around and rushed over to him as he lay curled up, holding his head. She rubbed his back, trying to soothe him as he cursed under his breath.

"Are you alright?" Lydia asked. Raiel continued lying on the bed curled up, not answering her. She continued rubbing his back, worried that he had made his head injury worse. She was just about to suggest again that they go to the hospital when he seemed to relax, and he removed his hands from his head. He slowly rolled onto his back, and Lydia averted her eyes. She really wished that he had at least been wearing underwear or had kept his pants on. She was just about to suggest that he put his jeans back on, when he reached up and pulled her to him.

"What are you doing?" Lydia asked. She tried to push him away, but he held her close and kissed her. She suddenly felt very scared of this man whom only a few hours before she nearly worshiped. Lydia struggled to pull away, but Raiel was incredibly strong. He pulled his mouth away from hers and smiled.

"You need to relax," Raiel said. "This is what we've both been wanting ever since you ran into me on the street."

"I think this is what *you've* wanted ever since we met, but not me. I thought you were a nice guy, and I was looking forward to getting to know you better. But now I don't think I want to know you at all."

"What? I thought there was something between us? Didn't you feel that spark between us when we met?"

"Yes, I felt something between us, but you're moving way too quickly. I don't hop into bed with a man on the first date, so let me go."

Lydia struggled against Raiel's grip, but it didn't loosen. If anything, she thought it got tighter.

"I don't understand. I thought we were attracted to each other. Isn't this the next logical step in our relationship?"

"No! What planet are you from anyway? This isn't how a relationship is supposed to work. We're supposed to get to know each other and develop a friendship and trust first. Then it can move to sex *if* we're both ready for it. Sometimes things move faster, but both parties have to be ready for it, and I'm definitely not ready for it."

"So you've just been leading me on this whole time?"

"No. I was interested in getting to know you better, but I never led you on. Now let me go. You're scaring me."

Raiel just held her, not loosening his grip at all. He had a look of confusion on his face, like he was trying to process everything that was going on.

"You're lying," Raiel said. "You wanted it as badly as I did, and now you're changing your mind."

"Why are you doing this?" Lydia asked. "I thought you were a good guy, but apparently I was mistaken."

"I *am* good," Raiel said. "I just want to be with you and have you by my side in the coming days."

"Oh my God," Lydia said, as she stared at Raiel in disbelief. Father Stephens' warnings suddenly rang out in her mind. "Father Stephens was right. You're the dark angel he warned me about."

"What?" Raiel asked. "I'm not the fallen one; Jetrel is. He's the one trying to destroy the world—not me. I'm trying to stop him."

"Father Stephens told me that you would lie to me, and that I would have to make a decision about which of you to follow. I thought he was crazy, but he was telling the truth."

"You must follow me," Raiel said. "Jetrel is evil and will destroy you along with the rest of the world."

"I won't believe anything you tell me," Lydia said. "I don't know who Jetrel is, but I would take his word over yours!"

Raiel threw Lydia to the floor and then pounced on her, his anger finally reaching its limit. He sat on her chest, pinning her arms to her sides. She tried to scream, but he clamped his hand painfully over her mouth. With the other, he started pulling drawers out of her dresser and dumping the contents on the floor until he found a ball of socks. He removed his hand from her mouth and stuffed it with the rolled-up socks. He took a pair of panty hose and tied them around her mouth to keep her from spitting the socks out. Then he got up and dragged her to the bed by her hair.

Lydia struggled against Raiel, but he outweighed her by a great deal and was much stronger. She hit him several times, but he didn't seem to notice. He pulled her shirt off over her head and tossed it aside. He slid down to unbutton her jeans and she saw her opportunity. When he leaned his head down, she closed her fist and swung it against the side of his head with all the strength she could muster.

Raiel screamed and tumbled sideways off the bed. Lydia grabbed her shirt and ran for the front door. She pulled her shirt on, ran into the hallway to the apartment across from hers, and began pounding on the door. She tore the panty hose off her head and pulled the rolled-up socks from her mouth while she waited. When the elderly man opened the door, she nearly knocked him over as she pushed her way into his apartment. She slammed the door behind her and locked the dead bolt.

"What are you doing?" the old man asked. He looked frightened, but Lydia was sure that it was nothing compared to what she was feeling. Without answering him, she grabbed the phone and dialed 911. She waited anxiously for someone to pick up on the other end, while watching the front door. She hoped the police would be able to get there before Raiel was able to get out of her apartment. The last thing she needed was another crazy man stalking her.

CHAPTER 25 - FATHER STEPHENS

Father Stephens paced up and down the center aisle of the church, unable to sit down or relax. He hadn't heard from either Raiel or Jetrel since they had left in search of the key, and he was beginning to worry. It was getting late in the evening, and he had expected some word from one or the other. He knew Jetrel was upset with him, but figured he would at least have stopped by to gloat about the fact that he now had the key and that they had failed to stop him. Even if he didn't, the locusts swarming the Earth would have indicated his success.

Father Stephens walked to the front doors to stand outside and look out for Raiel or Jetrel. It was something he had started doing to break the monotony of pacing. Before he reached the doors, one of them opened, and Raiel stumbled through it and collapsed. Father Stephens ran to him and rolled him onto his back. Raiel looked up at him and smiled.

"It's good to see you, Father."

"From the looks of you, you're lucky to be seeing anything." Father Stephens looked down at all the bruises and bandages on Raiel's body. He had obviously been in a very intense battle, but had apparently had enough time to treat all his wounds.

"The battle didn't go well."

"Did you get the key?" Father Stephens didn't even realize he was holding his breath as he waited for the answer, but when Raiel shook his head, the priest finally began breathing again. It definitely wasn't the answer he wanted, but as long as Raiel was alive, then there was hope.

"I didn't get the key," Raiel said, "but I don't think Jetrel did either. We fought and, in the end, were both injured. Jetrel's going to have to go to the hospital for his wounds, which should buy us some time. There was an old vagrant with him, but I don't think he's sober enough to finish digging up the key. They seem to be friends, so he will probably try to get

Jetrel some help as soon as he can. At least now I know the key's location, and once I am strong enough, I'll go back to retrieve it."

"You're in no shape to be going after the key. You need to rest and regain your strength."

"This is no time to be resting, Father. I need to find that key or else all humanity will suffer. If Jetrel gets to the key first, then all will be lost."

Father Stephens stood and helped Raiel to his feet. He led the angel to the basement stairs and helped him down them. There was a fold-out cot on which he had been sleeping since all the madness had begun. It wasn't a very comfortable bed, but it was better than the concrete floor.

Raiel lay back on the cot and moaned. He started gently rubbing the right side of his head, where Father Stephens could see a large and particularly nasty bruise forming. He went to the kitchen and made an ice pack using a plastic bag and an old kitchen towel. He carried the ice pack to Raiel, who accepted it with thanks and placed it against the side of his head.

"Raiel," Father Stephens said. "Why don't you tell me where the key is and I'll go find it for you?"

"What?" Raiel asked. "That's crazy. What if you run into Jetrel?"

"I don't think the fallen one will hurt me, and if what you told me is true, he won't be there. If you tell me where to search, I can get to the key before Jetrel recovers enough to go after it."

Raiel sighed and adjusted the ice pack against his head. It was obvious that he didn't like the idea, but he seemed to be having trouble thinking of a reason not to go along with it.

"Fine," Raiel said. "You'll need a good lantern, a shovel, and maybe a pickax if you can find one."

Father Stephens grabbed a notebook from his desk and started writing down all the directions as Raiel gave them to him. It sounded as if it would be a long trip, but not a tremendously difficult one. He left Raiel to rest and recuperate on his cot while he went upstairs to lock up the church.

He stopped by his house and changed into an old tee shirt, jeans, and sneakers. He didn't want to get his good clothes dirty, and he needed to pick up some money to purchase the supplies. He left the house and went to a hardware store, where he bought a small battery-operated lantern like the one Raiel had told him about. He then bought a shovel and a small pickax to help him remove the rocks from the tunnel floor. Then he left the store with his supplies in hand and headed into the slums.

Even with the directions Raiel had given him, it took Father Stephens a while to find the right building. All the old buildings in that part of town looked similar. When he finally found the right one, he went to the small window in the alley and opened it. He wriggled through the window, nearly getting stuck. He pushed against the window frame, trying to force himself through. If he survived this whole ordeal, he swore that he would go on a diet and stick to it this time. He sucked in his gut as much as he could and finally managed to force himself through. He stood and picked up the shovel, pick, and lantern, which he had pushed through ahead of him. He clicked on the lantern and saw several transients sitting around the sales floor of the old store. They were all watching him in amazement, but none of them made any sort of move toward him, so he assumed he was safe.

Father Stephens headed to the storeroom and descended the stairs inside. He reached the small room that Raiel had told him about and opened the old steel door. He took a deep breath and headed into the darkness.

He walked through the tunnels, passing the niche in the wall that a vagrant had made his home, but he saw no one there. He continued past the niche and headed deeper into the tunnels. He had trouble following the path Raiel had told him to take, because the directions had been rather vague. Raiel had followed some sixth sense that had directed him to the key, so he hadn't really paid too much attention to the path he had taken. Luckily for Father Stephens, Raiel and probably Jetrel had left a trail of footprints and blood that nearly anyone could follow. The directions had gotten him as far as they needed to; now all he had to do was follow the trail in front of him.

Father Stephens reached the hole in the stone floor and set his lantern down. A shovel and baseball bat lay forgotten on the floor, but there was no sign of Jetrel or the man who had apparently been with him. Father Stephens used his pickax to start chipping away at the mortar around the stones. He didn't know how long it took, but he felt like he had been there for hours chipping away at the floor, throwing rocks onto the pile next to him. Once he felt the hole was big enough, he took up the shovel and started to dig at the packed earth that lay below the stone.

The dirt wasn't much easier to move than the stones had been. It was tightly packed and full of rocks. He worked the dirt loose and scraped it free of the hole. He had dug nearly three feet through the dirt before his shovel hit something. He dropped to his hands and knees and brushed the dirt off a stone box. He used his pickax to scrape the dirt from around the box until he got a good handhold and was able to force it out of the dirt. He set the box on his lap and looked at it.

The box was made completely out of stone and was about two feet by three feet. There were no carvings or writing of any sort on the outside, and he didn't even see a seam where the lid could be lifted off. He cleaned the dirt off as best he could and then ran his fingers gently over the surface. He tried to find some sort of latch or release, but he couldn't find anything. The box appeared to be made of solid stone. He wondered who had found the key and created this box for it, but he pushed the thought from his mind. There would be time to think about that later. Right now, he needed to get the box out of there before anything happened to it.

Father Stephens lifted the box, tucked it under his arm, and stood up. He debated taking his new tools with him, but didn't know how he would carry them along with the box and lantern. He picked up the lantern and left the shovel and pick behind.

Father Stephens followed the trail of blood and footprints back to the old store, made his way up the stairs, and struggled to squeeze through the window again. He managed to force himself through and picked up the box. Then he headed back to the church, hoping that all this would soon be over.

CHAPTER 26 - JETREL

Jetrel woke from a series of bizarre dreams about the world after the key of the Abyss was used by the demons. It was a place of nightmares and horrors far greater than any he had ever imagined. The thought of a world like that would have been thrilling to him before, but now it made his stomach turn.

Jetrel tried to sit up, but the sharp pain in his chest drove him to lie down again. He groaned and ran his hand over his chest, feeling a tight bandage that had been wrapped around it. He opened his eyes and looked around. He was in an old building of some sort, but it wasn't the old clothing store.

"Where the hell am I?"

"Oh," Sam said from somewhere nearby. "You're awake. That's a good thing 'cause I was starting to worry about you."

"What happened?" Jetrel asked. He rolled onto his good side and forced himself to sit up, despite the pain it entailed.

"Well, I hit that guy that attacked us with the baseball bat, and he hightailed it out of there. After that, I dragged you back to my place and laid you on my bed while I went and got help."

"What kind of help?"

"Well, I went and found Lucas. He's a pretty good guy. He was a medic in Vietnam. Anyway, I took him to my place, where he wrapped up your chest nice and tight. It should help your ribs heal quicker as long as you don't go getting into any more fights for a while."

"Where am I at? This doesn't look like the clothing store."

"Oh, we took you back to Lucas' place. I didn't want to leave you in the tunnels in case that guy came back to finish the job. I can handle myself in a fight, but this guy looked like he knew his way around a brawl too. Plus I'm not quite as young as I used to be, so I figured you'd be safer if I took you someplace else."

"I need to get back there," Jetrel said. He tried standing up but couldn't. "What if the angel goes back and finds the key before I do?"

"No, you don't need to go anywhere," Sam said. He put his hand on Jetrel's shoulder and held him down. "You need to stay here and rest for a while. That young kid ain't gonna be going anywhere for a while—not with the whuppin' I gave him. His ears'll be ringing for a week."

Sam started laughing, then pulled the flask from his coat and offered it to Jetrel, who took the bottle and drank deeply from it. He would have preferred some kind of painkiller, but the whiskey would have to do for now. He handed the bottle back to Sam, who took another drink before slipping it back into his coat pocket.

"How long have I been out?" Jetrel asked.

"A few hours," Sam said. "It's about ten o'clock in the evening right now, but you shouldn't be worrying about the time. What you need to be doing is resting. Why don't you just lie back down and go to sleep? In the morning, we can go see about your key."

Jetrel nodded and lay back down. He didn't want to stay there and wait to get better. He needed to find the key before Raiel did. He wasn't sure what he'd do with the key when he found it, but he would worry about that when the time came. Sam was right about one thing, though—he was in no shape to be going anywhere. And if Sam had given Raiel the beating he said he had, then Raiel wouldn't be going after the key tonight either. So with little else to do, Jetrel closed his eyes and went to sleep.

The next day, he awoke with the sun shining through a broken window directly into his eyes. He covered his face with his arm and started to roll over, but the pain in his side stopped him. He sat up slowly and looked around. They were in a building that must have been some sort of warehouse at one time. There was debris scattered all across the floor, which he was beginning to suspect was common in all abandoned buildings.

Jetrel saw Sam sleeping on the floor a short distance from the old mattress that had been serving him as a bed. He found himself growing quite fond of the old man. If it hadn't been for Sam, Raiel would have killed him back in the tunnel.

He never would have suspected that an angel could kill someone so readily, but he saw the look of bloodlust in Raiel's eyes. He had killed before and would do it again now that he had a taste for it. Jetrel knew that feeling of power. It was the same feeling he used to get when he drew a soul from the flames to deal out a little one-on-one torment. It was like a drug, and now that Raiel had a taste for it, he was even more dangerous.

Jetrel stood up slowly. He walked over to Sam and nudged the old man with his foot. Sam woke with a start, looking around wildly. When he saw Jetrel standing above him, he calmed down and sat up.

"What the hell do you think you're doing scaring an old man like that?" Sam asked. "You could have given me a heart attack. Then what would you do without me around to pull your ass out of the fire?"

"Somehow I think you're a lot tougher to kill than that," Jetrel said, smiling. He found himself smiling a lot more often lately, and it felt good. "I just wanted to wake you up so you wouldn't sleep the whole day away."

Sam got up and stretched, causing a series of bones to crack. He then shuffled over to the corner of the building and relieved himself. Jetrel shook his head and walked over to the broken window, where he waited for Sam to finish.

"What's on the agenda today?" Sam asked. "Are we going to go find that key thing you're looking for?"

"Yeah, I'd feel a lot better if I had it in my possession."

"Okay, but how about some breakfast first?"

"Am I buying?" Jetrel asked.

"Of course. I saved your bacon yesterday, so the least you can do is buy me some today."

Jetrel laughed and helped Sam through a broken window. Then he followed and they made their way to the small diner/weapon shop they had visited the day before.

Their breakfast was great, and the portions were incredible. Jetrel ate as much as he could and then passed his plate over to Sam, who wolfed the rest of it down. When they finished eating and paid the bill, they headed back to the tunnels.

Jetrel had trouble getting through the small window with his injured ribs, but Sam helped to pull him through from the other side. Jetrel stood up, rubbing his ribs, and followed Sam, who had already started for the old stockroom. His ribs still hurt, but not nearly as much as they had the previous day. His natural ability to heal rapidly was a blessing, but it took a lot longer to heal bones than it did to heal flesh.

Sam retrieved Jetrel's lantern from where he had hidden it the day before and turned it on. The two men went down the stairs and started toward the tunnel. As they passed by his domicile, Sam stopped to refill his flask from one of the larger bottles along the wall. Once that important task had been taken care of, they resumed their journey.

Jetrel got more nervous the farther they went through the tunnels. He had been trying to sense the key, but it seemed as if the signal was coming from behind them. He hoped that they weren't too late, but deep down, he knew that they were.

As they rounded the corner and saw that the hole they had started the day before was now much larger, Jetrel's heart sank. He had failed his mission; now Raiel had the key and there was no telling what he would do with it.

"Someone beat us to it," Sam said.

"You have a flair for stating the obvious," Jetrel said. "I knew that we should have come back last night instead of sleeping."

"Don't get your panties in a wad," Sam said. "You said that you can track that thing, right? Well, just put your nose to the ground and sniff it out. If what you said is true and the bad angel has it, then he must not have used it or else the Earth would be covered in a plague of locusts or whatever it was you said would happen. So I figure we've got time, as long as you don't spend too much of it standing around here feeling sorry for yourself."

Jetrel looked at him in amazement. He couldn't believe that the old man had the balls to talk to him that way. He was impressed. Plus what he'd said made a lot of sense. He needed to find out where the key was and whether or not Raiel had it.

"You're right, Sam," Jetrel said. "We've still got a shot at this thing, so we'd better get going."

Jetrel slapped Sam on the back and they headed back toward the store. If they could get to the key in time, he might be able to stop Raiel before he was able to use it for whatever purpose he had planned. Plus he had a score to settle with the angel, and when he got a hold of him, he would make sure that he paid the price.

CHAPTER 27 - RAIEL

Raiel lay on the cot in the church basement with the ice pack firmly planted against the side of his head. Things had not gone the way he had planned, and he was fuming. He failed to get the key and he failed to get Lydia. Now his only hope was that Father Stephens would be able to get the key and bring it to him. Maybe then he could go back to Heaven and everything would be forgiven. If he ever had the chance to come back to Earth in the future, he would refuse. Everything was horrible down here and everyone had their own agenda—even Lydia.

Raiel had stumbled through the streets, trying to remain conscious until he got to her. Once he'd gotten there, she'd led him on and then shot him down. She was nothing but a tease, and then to top things off, she'd hit him. He'd had to use all the strength he had not to pass out before he'd gotten out of the apartment and made it to the church.

Now he'd been left there by himself in misery.

Raiel made himself get out of bed and walk over to Father Stephens' small office. He looked over the papers on the desk and saw that he'd been researching the key and questioning why the demons would be so interested in it. He had wondered about that himself, but had no more answers than Father Stephens did. The only one who would really know why the demons wanted the key was Jetrel, and he doubted that the fallen one would be in a very conversational mood the next time he saw him.

Raiel went back to the cot and lay down again. His mind was now on the key and why it had all of a sudden become such an issue for everyone. As far as he knew, the demons couldn't do anything with it. The key's only purpose was for the fifth angel to loose the plague of locusts upon the Earth, and that would be pointless. They didn't actually kill people—just tormented them. Then, after the five-month period, it would be over.

Raiel closed his eyes and tried to put the whole issue of the key out of his mind. What he needed now was to sleep and to heal so that he would be at his best in case Jetrel tried to take the key from him. He felt himself drifting off to sleep, sure that when he next opened his eyes, he would see Father Stephens with the key of the Abyss.

Raiel woke up the next morning feeling much better than he had the night before. The pain in his head had subsided to a dull ache, and most of his bruises and wounds had faded to nearly nothing. He sat up and looked around for Father Stephens, but didn't see anyone. He went to the kitchen and ate a meager breakfast from the few items in the fridge. He was starting to worry that something might have happened to the priest, so he went upstairs to see if he was there, but all he found was an empty room. He went to the front doors and unlocked them. He stepped outside and looked around. The morning was brisk, but the sunshine made it bearable. He went back inside and got his jacket, deciding to go to the tunnels to see what had happened.

Raiel had walked nearly halfway to the tunnels when he stopped. The compass in his head wasn't pointing toward the tunnels anymore, but in a different direction entirely. He stood, wondering what had happened. He had a bad feeling that something had happened to the priest in his search for the key and wondered whether or not he should go to the tunnels to look for him. He debated this for a moment before deciding to go after the key. If something had happened to Father Stephens, then there was nothing he could do for him now. The key was more important. If it had fallen into Jetrel's hands, then the whole world was in danger.

Raiel turned away from the tunnels and started walking in the direction of the key. He had gone several blocks before he realized that the key was moving. He turned around to match the direction in which the key was moving, but it continued to change direction and speed. Whoever had the key was in a vehicle of some sort and was moving away from his location. The only one he could see doing that would be Jetrel; but if Jetrel had the key, why hadn't he returned to Hell with it? If part of the demon's plan for the key involved something here on Earth, there would still be time to stop him.

Raiel walked to the street and flagged down a cab. The cab driver pulled over and Raiel got in.

"Where to, buddy?" the cab driver asked.

"I'm not sure yet," Raiel said. "I'll just need you to drive in the direction I tell you to. Start out going north then I'll tell you where to go from there."

"Listen, man," the cab driver said, "I don't know what kind of games you're playing, but I'm not going to drag you all across town on some wild goose chase unless I see some cash up front. I've got better things to do with my time."

"No you don't; you're a cab driver," Raiel said. He dug in his pocket, pulled out several twenties, and slid them through the small sliding glass window. The cab driver picked them up and held each up to the light, trying to tell whether or not the money was real. He folded the bills and put them in his front shirt pocket, apparently certain enough that they were real. He started the meter and headed toward the north side of town.

Raiel sat in the back of the cab, giving the driver directions as he went. The cab driver, whose name plate said Ricky, followed the directions as best he could. He had to swing around a few one-way streets and take a couple of detours around construction, but all in all, he stayed on the path that Raiel told him to take. It took nearly an hour to find the rusty white car that his internal compass pointed to as the vehicle containing the key. They followed the car, which seemed to be driving around the city randomly. He was able to see that the driver was Father Stephens, but it was the passenger who caught him by surprise. The woman in the passenger seat was Lydia, and she appeared to be holding a box on her lap. It had to be the box containing the key of the Abyss, but he didn't understand why Lydia would have it. As far as he knew, she didn't even know Father Stephens, unless she had followed him when he'd left her apartment and gone to the church. If so, she'd probably told Father Stephens about what had happened, surely twisting the truth to make him look like the bad guy. If that was true, then he needed to get to Father Stephens and set the record straight. Then, if he still wouldn't hand the key over willingly, Raiel would have to take it by force. He couldn't risk it falling into Jetrel's hands.

When the car stopped at a red light, Raiel leapt from the cab and ran up to Father Stephens' car. He ignored the cab driver's shouts of protest. He had paid him far more than the fare would be, so he could just take it out of that. He opened the back door and jumped into the backseat. Father Stephens and Lydia both turned and looked at him.

"What are you doing here?" Father Stephens asked.

"I'm here for the key since you never brought it to the church last night. I thought something had happened to you, but apparently you just got some bad ideas put into your head by this devil woman next to you."

"Devil woman?" Lydia asked. "*You're* the one who attacked *me* last night, not the other way around."

"We were having an intimate moment when you freaked out and hit me across the face. I had to leave your apartment because I was worried about what you would do if I stayed."

Lydia looked from Raiel to Father Stephens in utter disbelief. Father Stephens continued driving, his hands tight on the wheel. He looked at Lydia and then back at Raiel. He had the look of a man who was torn. On the one hand, he trusted Lydia and believed her story. On the other hand, he had Raiel, an angel, who was supposed to be responsible for saving the world.

"Why don't you pull over, Father? We can try to figure this whole thing out," Lydia said.

"What's to figure out? I'm the chosen one. If you don't give the key to me, the world will be doomed."

Father Stephens said nothing. He simply pulled into the parking lot of a convenience store. He got out of the car and the other two passengers did the same. He walked over and took the box from Lydia. He started to turn back to Raiel, when he saw Jetrel walk out of the store. The dark angel's eyes went to the box Father Stephens was holding and then to Raiel.

CHAPTER 28 - LYDIA

Lydia sat in her apartment after dealing with the police for the second time in less than a week. After the police were on the way, she explained her situation to the old man, whose name she found out was Pete. After hearing her story, he softened up considerably and offered to get her some water. She accepted readily, her mouth dry from having the ball of socks stuffed inside it. After Pete got Lydia the water, he continued fussing over her until the cops showed up and knocked on the door.

Lydia met the cops in the hallway and let them into her apartment. Several officers went in and searched the place, but Raiel was nowhere to be found. One of the officers took her statement as well as that of her neighbor, even though he had only dealt with her after she'd fled. Lydia asked why so many officers had shown up, and one of them told her that the perpetrator fit the description of a man they were looking for. The man had allegedly assaulted an officer and stolen his clothing. Lydia told the officers that he had worn a police uniform on the night she had met him. She told them that the name tag on his uniform had said Officer Stillman. The policeman nodded, told her that it was the same guy they were looking for, and asked if she had any idea where he might have gone. She didn't know anything about him other than his name, which was what she told the officer.

The whole ordeal went on for nearly an hour. The cops questioned her repeatedly, trying to get new information about Raiel. She told them she didn't know anything else, but that didn't stop them from asking their questions. She dealt with it the best she could until they left and she was free to return to her apartment. She didn't want to stay there, but the cops said they would patrol the area and keep their eyes open. If she had any more problems with him, she was to call them immediately. The best thing she could do to protect herself was to keep the dead bolt locked and her eyes and ears open. She thanked them, even though the information was useless. These were things she already did, but it hadn't helped her that evening. Her problems that evening had been caused by her own stupidity.

Now she sat in her apartment watching TV and drinking coffee. Her whole body was on edge and she jumped at every noise. She watched through her window to see how often the cops patrolled her street, but it had been several hours and she had yet to see one drive by.

She got off her couch and took a nice warm shower before turning her TV off and heading to bed. She checked the dead bolt for the hundredth time and put a chair under the doorknob again. Then she went to bed and lay there listening to the sounds of her apartment, her heart pounding harder with each one. She didn't know how long it was before she fell asleep, but when she awoke, it was morning.

Lydia got up and showered again before making some coffee. She tried to eat something for breakfast but didn't really feel like it. Her nerves were shot, and she didn't think food would sit too well right now. Once she was dressed, she went outside, searching for any sign of Raiel. She secretly hoped that the cops had already gotten him, but she had her doubts. He had eluded the cops once and could probably do it again.

Lydia started walking toward the church where she had met Father Stephens, watching over her shoulder the whole way. Raiel was probably a long way from there, but she still couldn't shake the feeling that he was following her. When she reached the old church, Lydia found the doors locked. She sighed and sat down on the front steps. She didn't know why she had decided to go to Father Stephens about her troubles. Heck, she hardly even knew him, but she felt like all this might have something to do with what he had told her the other night.

Lydia had just about decided to leave when she saw Father Stephens coming down the sidewalk. He was carrying a small stone box under one arm and was sweating profusely. When he saw her, he smiled and waved. Lydia smiled and waved back. He managed to make it to the steps of the church and set the stone box down before sitting next to her. He was breathing heavily and sweat was running down from the top of his head to his face. Lydia dug through her purse, pulled out several napkins, and offered them to him. He thanked her and used them to mop the sweat from his face and head.

Once he had caught his breath, he turned toward Lydia and smiled again.

"So, to what do I owe this honor?" Father Stephens asked. "After our last conversation, I assumed I'd never see you again."

"Honestly, that's what I thought too, but strange things have happened to me lately and I'm starting to feel like it has something to do with what you told me."

"Well, fill me in, child, while I sit here and rest."

Lydia started her story from the beginning, telling him everything from the night of the first attack up until that point. When she had finished her story, she glanced over at Father Stephens, who looked pale and was hugging the stone box to his chest. He looked like he was in shock, but Lydia didn't think that her story could have caused that sort of reaction.

"Are you alright, Father?"

"I'm not sure," Father Stephens said. "Are you sure the man you told me about was named Raiel?"

"Yes, I'm positive."

"Then that's truly bad news," Father Stephens said. He turned to Lydia and began telling her his story. She listened to the whole thing and by the end, she was nearly as pale as he had been when she'd finished her story.

"So what does this mean?" Lydia asked. "If Raiel's gone off the deep end, then how can we ever give him the key? We don't know what he's capable of. Then again, we can't give it to Jetrel 'cause we don't know what his objectives are either. If Heaven and Hell are both sending angels to find this key, then I don't think we'll be able to protect it for very long."

"I know, child," Father Stephens said. "Those are the same questions I've been turning around in my mind. If we give the key to Raiel, will he be able to return to Heaven with it if he's committed sins? If Jetrel's truly repented, could he manage to get the key to Heaven even though he was cast out with Lucifer and the rest of his fallen angels? Those are the questions we must answer. Now I know what my visions mean, but the only problem is that we don't know which man will turn out to be the dark figure and which will be the figure of light. And until we know more, I don't believe we can safely give the key to either of them."

"So what are we supposed to do? If they can sense the key, then they'll be able to find it no matter where we hide it."

Father Stephens and Lydia sat on the church steps in silence for several minutes before either of them came up with an idea.

"I think," Father Stephens said, "that we should get in my car and drive around the city. As long as we're not sitting in one spot, they shouldn't be able to pinpoint the key's exact location. That should give us some time to try to figure out what to do next."

"That's a lot better than any of my ideas," Lydia said. "I think we better hurry, though, before either one comes in search of the key."

Father Stephens nodded and got up. He put the box under his right arm and walked to his car, praying that his plan would buy them the time they needed.

CHAPTER 29 - JETREL

Jetrel started walking in the direction in which the key was pulling him, followed closely by Sam. The two men had nearly reached the source when it began moving. Jetrel stood on the sidewalk, puzzled. He figured that the key had to be in a car or some other sort of vehicle, based on how it was moving. What he didn't know was why Raiel would be in a car and what he was planning to do with the key. He could tell by the look in his eyes that Raiel had snapped, which made it nearly impossible to try to sort out what he was planning.

"The key's moving," Jetrel said. "He must be in a car, but I have no idea where he would be going."

"We need to find a car of our own and follow him," Sam said.

"I don't have one, do you?" Jetrel asked.

"Nope, and that's one thing I don't know how to get."

"Maybe we'll have to borrow one."

"That I can do," Sam said. He walked over to a nearby car and looked it over. He reached into his coat pocket, pulled out some rubber gloves, and tossed a pair to Jetrel, who reluctantly put them on while looking around to see if anyone was watching. Sam took a rock from off the ground and smashed in the driver's side window. A car alarm started blaring, but Sam opened the door, got inside, and reached beneath the dash. He pulled out several wires, yanked several of them from the dash, and the alarm stopped. Then he reached over, unlocked the door, and Jetrel quickly climbed in. Sam was pulling more wires out of the dash until he found the ones he was looking for. He tapped them together and the car started. He sat back up, put the car into drive, and tore off down the street.

"Is there anything you don't know how to do?" Jetrel asked.

"There's plenty I don't know, but plenty I do know too. Not all of us bums are good for nothing. Some of us actually have brains and know how to use them."

"Luckily, I ran into one of them," Jetrel said.

Sam nodded and continued driving. Jetrel gave him directions the best he could, and Sam was very good at following them. They drove in circles around the city as the car containing the key did its best to lose them.

"We're getting close," Jetrel said.

They were nearing the key when their car suddenly died. Sam steered it to the edge of the road and got out.

"What happened?" Jetrel asked. He climbed out of the car and began following Sam as he started walking down the sidewalk.

"We ran out of gas," Sam said. "It's my fault; I was paying more attention to your directions than I was to the gas gauge." Sam pulled off his gloves and put them into his pocket; Jetrel did the same. They walked through several residential areas before finding a convenience store. They needed to find another car before they lost the key or Raiel went through with his plan. Sam went into the convenience store to use the restroom, while Jetrel bought a couple of pops for them. They needed to think of a new plan—and quickly. Jetrel had just finished paying when he noticed that the signal was very close. He saw a white car outside and watched while Father Stephens and the woman he had saved the first night he was on Earth got out. Then he saw Raiel get out of the backseat. Jetrel headed out the door, leaving his drinks on the counter. Father Stephens had taken the box from the woman, and Jetrel watched it intently. He knew that it contained the key and that Father Stephens was about to hand it over to Raiel.

Jetrel drew his gaze away from the box and looked at Raiel. He didn't know what was going on, but he did know that if he didn't do something quickly, he would lose the key.

"So are all three of you in on this together?" Jetrel asked.

"No, I found the key, but took it until I could figure out which one of you to give it to," Father Stephens said.

"What do you mean?" Raiel asked. "There shouldn't be any question about it. I'm the one that was sent to save humanity from the chaos that Jetrel and his kind want to bring to Earth. I need to get the key and return it to Heaven before it's too late."

"You're nothing more than a cold-blooded killer now," Jetrel said. "Giving the key to you would be just as devastating as handing it over to Satan himself."

"Stop it, both of you!" Lydia said. "I don't think either of you should have the key. What's to say that we can't keep it and protect it ourselves?"

"The key will never be safe as long as it's here on Earth," Raiel said. "It needs to be with the archangels in Heaven and, therefore, it should go to me."

"I think that Father Stephens is right," Jetrel said. "Why don't we let them keep it until they can determine which of us to give it to?"

"That's ridiculous," Raiel said. "The answer should be obvious. They shouldn't have to think about whom to give it to. I'm the only one of us who can take the key to Heaven where it will be protected by an army of archangels."

"No," Father Stephens said. "I'm going to keep the key until I decide what to do with it."

"You can't do that," Raiel said. "I'm the only logical choice. Even if Jetrel has changed, he could never get the key to Heaven where it belongs. The only place he can go is back to Hell. If he tries to stay on Earth and hide the key, then other demons will be sent to find him and take the key."

"I'm sorry, Raiel," Father Stephens said. "I'm going to keep the box."

"Well, if there's only one of us, then you'll have only one choice about who to give it to," Raiel said. He ran toward Jetrel and punched him across the face. Father Stephens and the young woman got into the car and started it. Raiel turned to go after them, but Jetrel caught him by his shirt and pulled him back. Father Stephens drove away as Raiel turned to Jetrel.

Jetrel hit Raiel, but it didn't seem to have much effect. Raiel was completely submerged in a blind rage and was feeling no pain. Raiel hit Jetrel, knocking him into the side of the convenience store. He stood back up just in time to duck another swing from Raiel and land one of his own. He tried to slip away, not wanting to get pinned against the building, but Raiel caught him and threw him into the ice cooler. Jetrel's gun was knocked from the back of his jeans and clattered against the concrete. Both men looked at it momentarily before trying to grab it.

Raiel got the gun first, but before he could use it, Jetrel knocked it from his grasp. Raiel turned to go after it, and Jetrel hit him in the back with a hard shot to the kidney. Raiel straightened up, grasping at his back, and Jetrel went for the gun. Raiel tripped him and then kicked him in his injured ribs several times before grabbing the gun. He turned to Jetrel, not worrying about the consequences. The priest wouldn't give him the key, so he would have to take it from him and he couldn't do that with Jetrel trailing after him like a lost puppy.

Jetrel stood up, clutching at his ribs. He had hoped to try to get the gun from Raiel, but with his aching ribs, he could barely move. Jetrel closed his eyes, accepting his fate, as Raiel pulled the trigger. The report was deafening, but Jetrel didn't feel the bullet strike him. He opened his eyes and saw Sam standing in front of him. Raiel stared at the old man who had taken the bullet for Jetrel. They had been right all along; he was a murderer. Raiel looked at the gun in his hand and staggered backward. He looked at the bleeding man standing in front of him, tossed the gun aside, and then turned and ran from the scene.

Jetrel stepped up and caught Sam as he fell backwards. He lowered him slowly to the sidewalk. Jetrel took his coat off and covered him with it. Sam looked up at him in disbelief, which was what Jetrel was feeling as well.

"Why did you do that?" Jetrel asked.

"Are you kidding?" Sam asked. "I had to pull your ass out of the fire again. If I didn't do it, no one would. Then where would you be?"

"You should have let me die. I lied to you. I'm not the good angel; Raiel is. I just wanted you to help me, and I didn't think you would if you knew what I really was. That's why you should have let me take the bullet." Jetrel's voice had started to take on a panicked tone as he realized that Sam was slipping away from him. He had been the only true friend he had ever had, and he couldn't stand to think that he was about to die because of him. He wiped at the tears that were streaming down his face and looked into Sam's eyes.

"It doesn't matter…what you were when you got here," Sam said. His breathing was starting to get shallow, and he was having difficulty talking. "The only thing that matters…is what you are now… I've seen what kind of…person you are inside…and that man is anything but evil… You need to learn that you're…as good as anyone else on Earth…and you can make a difference… Now go and get that key…and do whatever you have to…to save the world…" Sam reached up to his neck, grabbed the cross that he had tied there, and yanked it, breaking the string. He handed the cross to Jetrel, who took it by the string and dropped it into his pocket before the cops arrived.

"That's the…only thing…of value…I have," Sam said. "I want…you to…have it…and wear it…proudly…" Jetrel knelt there over his friend, crying as the life slipped from Sam's body. He had lost his only friend, and he made a promise to himself that it wouldn't be in vain. He would get the key and make sure that Hell would never get hold of it.

CHAPTER 30 - FATHER STEPHENS

Father Stephens and Lydia drove from the scene as quickly as they could. They knew that the battle would be bloody, and they didn't want to be around to find out which of the two angels won and tried to claim the prize. So they drove, not really knowing where they were going.

"That guy Jetrel was the one who saved me that night when I was nearly raped and killed," Lydia said. "He was the one we should have given the key to."

Father Stephens didn't reply. He still wasn't sure which one of them to give the key to, no matter how strongly Lydia felt. It wasn't a matter of whom they could trust; it was a matter of who could get the key to Heaven and safely out of the reach of Satan. He didn't believe that Jetrel, no matter how good he was, would be able to do that. He was a demon, and when he had the key, he would only be able to return to Hell with it. That was how it worked, and no matter how many good deeds he did, he couldn't make it otherwise.

The two rode in silence from then on, neither knowing what to say to the other. Father Stephens had no idea where he was driving to, so he just continued to drive. He would turn occasionally, just to make sure that they couldn't be easily tracked.

Less than a week before, he never could have guessed that his life would lead him to this point. Yet there he was, on the run with a young stripper, trying to keep a magical key away from two angels. It was the reason he had been having visions and had been spending all his time in the church. That church had always been his second home, and for the past week, it had been his actual home. It was where he had met Raiel, Lydia, and Jetrel. It was the one place where he felt the safest, so he figured that it would be the best place to protect the key.

Father Stephens turned the car onto a side street and started heading back toward the church. After a few minutes, he pulled up in front of the building and looked at Lydia.

"I think it's time to stop running and start making some tough decisions."

Lydia nodded and handed him the stone box. He took it from her and they both got out of the car and walked up to the church. They walked through the front doors, each feeling a heavy tension in the air. They knew that the final battle would be taking place soon, and all they could do was wait for it to begin.

Father Stephens walked to the altar and set the box upon it. When the box touched the altar, runes began to glow on the outside, and a crack appeared along the top of it. He and Lydia looked at each other, both unsure of what to do. Father Stephens reached out and took hold of the top of the box. He lifted gently and the lid slid off. Once the lid was off, the stone stopped glowing and resumed its previous appearance.

Father Stephens and Lydia leaned over the box and looked inside. Lying upon a silken pillow, finer than anything either of them had ever seen, was the key.

It was a black skeleton key, nearly a foot long. The teeth looked like jagged fangs, and a black demonic wing made up the other end. It was a hideous monstrosity.

Without thinking, Lydia reached out and took the key in her hand. Father Stephens started to tell her not to, but she had picked it up too quickly. The key began humming softly in her hand, and she walked with it to the middle of the church. She lifted the key up above her head, and it started to glow. It was incredibly bright, and soon a glow started at her feet as well. The glow brightened to near blinding before fading. When Father Stephens looked at Lydia, he saw that she was standing upon a large circle that was glowing on the floor. The circle was covered with runes and long-forgotten holy symbols. At the center of the circle was a glowing keyhole. Lydia stepped toward the hole and brought the key toward it.

Father Stephens shouted for her to stop, and he ran toward her. He grabbed Lydia and pulled her away from the circle. He took the key from her hand and, while averting his eyes from both the key and the circle on the floor, walked back up to the box. He set the key atop the pillow and put the lid on the box.

Once the lid was in place, the circle faded from the floor, and Lydia blinked and rubbed her eyes as if waking from a deep sleep.

"What happened?" Lydia asked.

"You were under the key's spell, and you used it to bring forth the gate of the Abyss. You nearly opened it."

"I'm sorry, Father. I didn't realize what was happening."

"That's okay. I think this key is far too powerful for either of us to wield. It's probably better if we leave it in the box."

The box on the altar continued to glow, so Father Stephens covered it with a tablecloth from downstairs. Then he and Lydia sat down to wait for the end game to start.

CHAPTER 31 - RAIEL

Raiel ran from the convenience store, trying to find a place to hide until everything had a chance to blow over. He didn't know whether or not the sirens he heard in the distance were coming to the convenience store, but it was only a matter of time.

He had killed again; but this time, it hadn't been someone he'd intended to kill. It's true that the man had beaten him senseless with a baseball bat, but Raiel hadn't meant to kill him. Was he truly a monster, or was all this a necessary part of the job he had been sent to do? He wished there were someone he could talk to about it, but Father Stephens would probably never talk to him again.

Raiel made his way downtown, which was the area he knew the best. He found an unoccupied alley and sat down in the shadows to wait. Lately, he had spent a lot of time in dark alleys. They were the only places where he felt safe. He was a being of light, yet only the darkness brought him comfort. It seemed to be the way of life in the city. The city's front was one of false cheer, which showed itself through the brightly lit displays set up in the storefronts that lined the streets. The people walking these streets also had their displays set up. They smiled and talked in friendly tones with the people they encountered, each one doing their best to make the other one think that the sun was up and everything was right with the world.

But each building and person had their own alley, where few dared to walk. It was in these alleys that the darkness lay, whether in the form of gangs that hid in the darkness to rob and murder, or the dark impulses that hid within everyone's minds. These were impulses that they would never want anyone to discover, but they were held by so many others around them. Most didn't act upon them, but when they did, that was when the alleys of the city became dangerous.

Raiel believed that he was now one of those dangers. This world had driven him to everything he had done and he hated it. Actually, it wasn't the world itself, but the people in it.

He had only one mission to accomplish, but these humans stood in his way at every turn. They were everywhere, each one seemingly determined to stop him. He hated them for their incompetence and stupidity, both of which made them dangerous to everyone around them. The intelligent ones were few and far between and were restricted by the fumbling brethren surrounding them. It was the dull-witted ones and those who followed the dark impulses who had driven him to kill. He had to do what was needed to find the key, and if he hadn't, then he might have been the one who'd been killed.

Raiel sat in the shadow of a large dumpster for several hours, running these thoughts through his mind, slowly convincing himself that he was just in his actions. He was doing God's work, and everything he did was in God's name.

He knew his actions were just, but they might not appear as such if he failed to acquire the key. In that case, the sacrifices those men had made would have been for nothing. He had to get the key before Jetrel could claim it, if he hadn't already. It was clear that Father Stephens and Lydia were under Jetrel's influence, but that didn't mean that it was too late.

Raiel stood up and looked around before emerging and heading for the street. He looked around again before stepping out onto the sidewalk. He worried about looking suspicious, but more than likely, no one would notice since half of the people in the city walked around acting strangely. He was more worried about the cops, who all probably had his description by now. If they should see him and catch him before he could find the key, then Jetrel would be able to find it at his leisure while he sat behind bars. He couldn't let that happen.

Raiel headed down the sidewalk, trying to keep his head down. He would occasionally glance up to scan the streets for any sign of the police, but there had been none so far. He decided that he needed to head to the church since that was probably where they would take the key. He thought they might still be driving around, but didn't know. His mind was such a tangle of emotions that he couldn't concentrate enough to feel the key's presence. His best bet was to head to the church. If they weren't there, then he would have to wait until they showed up, or until he could calm himself enough to sense the key.

He noticed a police cruiser coming down the street toward him and suddenly became very interested in the fishing gear on display in the window next to him. He looked absently at the sign that read "Come in to Dave's Sporting Goods today and catch yourself a great deal!" It was a rather cheesy and cliché example of word play, of which Dave was probably very proud. It wasn't the sign that had caught his attention, though;

it was the reflection of the street behind him that he saw in the glass. He held his breath as the cruiser went slowly past him without stopping, letting it out only when he was sure the vehicle wasn't going to stop. He turned back to his path and headed for the church.

There were no other close calls with the police on the way to the church, and Raiel was thankful for that. There was never a cop around when you needed one, but the moment you didn't want one around, they seemed to be swarming through the streets like roaches.

Raiel rounded the street corner and saw the small church at the end of the block. He approached and circled to the back. He saw that Father Stephens' car was parked in the small graveled area just off the alley. He smiled and headed for the back door of the church. Now that he knew they were there, and that the key was probably inside, he was able to relax a little and finally began to sense the key's presence. It was inside the church, and since he didn't sense Jetrel, he assumed it was still safe. He swore to himself right then that he wouldn't leave the church without the key, no matter what he had to do to get it.

CHAPTER 32 - JETREL

Jetrel endured the endless questioning of the police as best he could, trying not to lose his temper. He needed to get out of there and find Father Stephens and Lydia. Raiel was undoubtedly in search of them, and it was only a matter of time before he found them. They could probably avoid him for a while, but in the end, he would find them. Then, if they wouldn't give up the box, he would probably be more than willing to kill them for it. He needed to find them first so he could help protect them. None of them knew what to do with the key, but keeping it away from Raiel was the one thing they could agree on.

The police had finished taking his statement as they were loading Sam's body into the ambulance. He had been pronounced dead, but his body had laid there covered in a sheet for several hours as the police had investigated the scene. He couldn't stand seeing Sam lying there on the concrete covered in the bloody sheet, but this was worse. He wasn't sure if he would ever see Sam's body again. Did they have funerals for the homeless, or were they simply buried? Perhaps a priest would say a few words as they laid the body to rest; but if the person had no real friends or family, what then? Sam had at least one true friend, and Jetrel told himself that if he survived this upcoming battle, he would find out where Sam's body was going and he would be there to give a eulogy.

Once the body was loaded and the ambulance left to take the corpse to the morgue, Jetrel turned away from the scene and headed toward the church. That was probably where Father Stephens had headed. It wasn't the smartest place to run to, but when people were scared or confused, their first impulse was to run to a comfortable place and hide. He hoped Raiel was hiding out until the heat was off, but he couldn't be sure of it. He was unstable, and Jetrel had no idea what he would be capable of anymore. And now that he had killed Sam...

Jetrel stopped and sat down on the curb. The thought of Sam sent another bout of grief coursing through him, and he felt as though he would faint. He sat there with his elbows on his knees and his face buried in his hands, and he started crying. He had never felt anything like this intense sadness, and he didn't know what to do about it other than cry. He sobbed uncontrollably for several minutes, not caring what anyone watching him would think. He had never cared for anyone before, and to have them ripped away from him so quickly was a torture worse than any he had felt before.

Jetrel checked his pockets for something to dry his face with and burned his hand on the cross that Sam had given him. He pulled the cross from his pocket and then tore the sleeves from his shirt and used them to dry his eyes. His tears had started to subside, and he was slowly starting to regain his composure.

"Why does life on Earth have to be so hard?" he asked of no one in particular. He stared at the cross hanging from the string in his hand. There was so much on Earth that he didn't understand. There were so many good things in life, but thrown in amidst these were lots of horrible things, many of which he and his kind were responsible for. There were demons out there whose sole purpose was to corrupt humans, and they were good at it. He assumed there were angels out there whose jobs were to help people, but he didn't know for sure. Either way, there were many innocent people suffering needlessly. There were people out there who did their best to help those who suffered, but no matter how hard they tried, there was still so much darkness out there.

"It doesn't matter," Sam's voice said from the back of his mind. "It's not about winning or losing, it's about the battle. They may not be able to win the war, but if they didn't fight, they would surely lose. They go out every day and help those that they can, always knowing that it's a war they won't win. It doesn't matter that they can't save everyone, but to those they do save, it means everything. Now you can either sit here feeling sorry for yourself, or you can go save humanity from an eternity of torment.

"Besides, Father Stephens and Lydia are counting on you to save them, 'cause if you don't, then no one will. Once Raiel finds them, he'll kill them. Without you, they're as good as dead."

Jetrel blew his nose and tossed the small piece of cloth into the gutter. He wiped his face with the other piece and then stuck it in his pocket. Then he took the string and tied it around his neck, making sure that the cross was on the outside of his shirt. He looked down at the cross hanging there before getting up and walking again, this time toward downtown. He knew he needed to go to the church, but he had something else to do first.

Jetrel didn't know if the voice in his head was actually Sam or if it was just his own thoughts taking on the only voice of reason he had ever known. Either way, it spoke the truth and made him realize what was important. He had to finish this mission on his own because no one else would do it for him. He had to do what he felt was right and protect those who couldn't protect themselves.

Jetrel walked quickly, knowing he should be heading for the church, but first he needed to right a wrong that he had committed. He walked through downtown until he found the alley he was looking for. Before heading in, he looked around to make sure no one was watching. He walked over to a pile of garbage and began digging through it, worried that he was too late. He had started to consider giving up when he found the corpse of the puppy he had kicked into the wall. The puppy was an innocent too, and he had killed it when he should have helped it. It had no one to protect it, and he'd taken advantage of that. He was no better than any of the other scum who preyed on the weak, but at least he had the power make it right.

Jetrel took the body and held it against his chest. It was in bad shape and decomposition had started. It didn't matter. That only meant that he would have to put that much more of himself into it.

Jetrel closed his eyes and clutched the puppy's small form. He began singing softly and concentrating on the energy that was flowing from his body into the puppy's. The song was more of a prayer through which he was able to call upon the powers of light to draw the energy from his body and channel it into the puppy's. He began to sing more loudly, not caring whether or not anyone heard him. He felt the energy being drawn even faster, making his head swim and his body tingle like an appendage that had fallen asleep. The more he concentrated, the clearer the song became and the faster he was able to draw upon his memories. At first, he had struggled to remember the song, not having sung it since being cast out of Heaven after the great battle, but now it was flowing from him as if he had sung it every day.

Jetrel felt the life growing in the puppy as its body repaired itself. He was calling its soul to return to its vessel, while his energies prepared and restored the body. He felt the warmth return to the little body and its heart resume beating. He struggled to finish the song while his whole body burned and ached from the strain. He nearly screamed the last of it, trying to finish the song before his body gave out and collapsed.

When he finished, Jetrel fell onto his side to avoid injuring the puppy. He opened his arms and the puppy jumped free. It turned and looked at him as he struggled to regain his breath and waited for the world to stop spinning. Jetrel forced himself to look at the puppy and it looked back at him.

"I'm so sorry," Jetrel said. "Please forgive me."

The puppy started wagging its tail and licking Jetrel's face. He smiled and sat up. The puppy climbed onto his lap as Jetrel looked around the alley. He was surrounded by hundreds of black feathers swirling around the ground. He had spent an incredible amount of energy—way more than he should have, considering the battle he was facing. But if he hadn't done this, it would have haunted him. He wished that he could have used this power to help Sam, but bringing a human back was beyond his abilities.

"Come on," Jetrel said. "We need to go. We don't have much time."

The puppy jumped down and began to chase the feathers as Jetrel struggled to his feet. He started walking toward the church with the puppy trailing after him, a black feather in his mouth.

CHAPTER - 33 RAIEL

Raiel walked around the church, trying to open all the doors and windows, but they were all locked. He wanted to get in unnoticed and hoped that Father Stephens and Lydia had missed locking a window or two. He debated breaking out a window to gain access, but decided against it. It was broad daylight, and the breaking glass would almost certainly be heard by the occupants of the church. Instead, he figured that the direct approach would be best.

Raiel walked to the front of the church and pounded on the heavy oak doors. He stepped to the side a bit so that one of them would have to actually approach the window to see him. He soon saw Father Stephens' face at the window and he stepped back into view. The father took a sudden step back but didn't leave. It was a small blessing anyway, Raiel thought.

"I won't let you in," Father Stephens said. He stepped back up to the door, evidently realizing that Raiel wasn't going to try anything.

"What exactly are you planning to do with the key?" Raiel asked. "I don't think you have a lot of options."

"I will take the key away from here and protect it myself until my death, or until an angel is sent who is worthy of possessing the key."

Raiel felt his anger stir at the remark, but forced himself to keep his composure. He knew that he had ruined any chance of them trusting him, but perhaps he could still manage to persuade them to part with the key without resorting to violence.

"It doesn't matter whether or not you believe that I'm worthy. What matters is that I'm the only one that can return the key to Heaven where it can be protected. No matter how strongly you believe that Jetrel has changed, he's still one of the fallen, and he can't return to Heaven. I'm the only one who has any chance of getting the key there, which means that you have no other choice but to give it to me."

"I stand by my previous statement. I will not turn the key over to you or Jetrel. I will do everything in my power to hide it and protect it; I will not allow one who has been twisted by evil to touch such a holy relic."

"I have not been 'twisted by evil.' I have done only what I must to survive here on Earth, and it is not up to you to judge my merit." Raiel's voice began to rise along with his anger, both of which were climbing quickly. "Either open this door and allow me to take the key, or I will force it open and take the key by other means."

"I will not allow you into my church without a fight," Father Stephens said. His voice boomed with an authority that his face did not match. Raiel could see in his eyes that he was terrified. If he hadn't been able to see that fear, he may have second-guessed the father's ability to protect the key. What he saw now, however, was a man on the distant edge of his prime and in poor physical health. The key could probably be taken with little more than intimidation.

"If that's what it'll take for me to get the key to its rightful home, then that's what I'll do for the good of all humanity. I only hope that God will forgive you for the folly you are committing." Raiel turned and walked away from the door. He walked around to the side of the building. He grabbed a large edging stone from the flowerbed on his way and stopped in front of one of the large stained glass windows. He threw the rock against the glass and lifted his arm to shield himself from the colorful shards. The window gave way, sending glass crashing down both inside and outside the church. Raiel ran toward the window and threw himself through it before either of the building's occupants could react. He ignored the blades of glass that tore at his skin, and he quickly rolled to his feet. He barely even noticed the wounds he received. Right now, his mind was completely focused on the key.

Raiel had barely gotten up before he was struck by something and knocked back to the ground. He rolled to the side, barely able to avoid a second blow. He looked up at Lydia, who was swinging a large brass candlestick at him. He rolled aside again and grabbed the candlestick as it clanged harmlessly against the ground. Lydia tried to hang on to it, but couldn't match Raiel's strength. It was yanked roughly from her hands. She tried to push herself away from him, but couldn't. Raiel swung the candlestick at Lydia and caught her solidly in the ribs. A sudden, intense pain raced through her chest as several of her ribs snapped under the force of the swing.

Lydia fell to her knees, unable to breath, which gave Raiel the time he needed to regain his footing. He lifted the candlestick, intending to crush the back of Lydia's skull, when he felt a sharp pain across his back. The candlestick slid from his grasp and he turned to see that Father Stephens had decided to join the melee. He was swinging another brass candlestick, which Raiel was easily able to catch. He twisted the weapon from Father Stephens' grasp with his left hand and punched him with his right. Father Stephens dropped heavily to the floor and Raiel turned back to Lydia, only to find that she had crawled away. He started to go after her, but stopped and turned back to Father Stephens, who was unconscious. He debated finishing him off, but decided that the most important thing was for him to find the key. He tossed the candlestick aside and headed for the altar.

He sensed the key, and a feeling of euphoria overwhelmed him. The key seemed to sing to him, and it was one of the most beautiful things he had ever heard. He approached the stone box, pulled the tablecloth off, and gingerly touched it. The runes on the box hummed melodically. The song was so strong that it made his head swim. He gazed lovingly at the runes glowing on the stone box and gingerly traced them with his fingers. The runes told the story of the key contained within. They warned of its power and its potential, and that it was only to be used following the fifth sign of the Apocalypse. Raiel read all this, but none of it mattered. The only thing that mattered was that it was now his.

Raiel picked up the stone box and the runes immediately began to fade. He held it out in front of him carefully, like one would hold a bomb. He was scared to hold such an important artifact, afraid that one wrong move would cause it to break. Somewhere in his mind, he knew that the thought was ridiculous, but in his heart, he felt that this was the most important item in the world and that no amount of caution was too extreme. He pulled it to his chest, wrapped both his arms around it, and quickly started walking to the front door of the church.

As he got farther from the altar, a heavy sadness overcame him. He never wanted the beautiful melody to end, never wanted to give up the beautiful song he had heard. It reminded him of Heaven. He was thinking about turning around and putting the box back on the altar to hear the song again, when his foot caught on something and he fell.

Raiel cursed as the stone box slipped from his arms, but he could do nothing as it crashed heavily to the ground, reverberating across the entire church floor. Raiel turned and saw Lydia crawling toward the front of the church. He couldn't believe that the little bitch would have the nerve to trip him, but he was also grateful since the fall had managed to break the spell that the box seemed to have had over him.

Raiel crawled to the box and picked it up. He stood and turned toward Lydia. He would crush her head with the box and then do the same to Father Stephens. That would put an end to them and their meddling. He started walking toward Lydia when a large crash from behind him knocked him off his feet.

CHAPTER - 34 JETREL

Jetrel walked toward the church as quickly as he could, and the newly risen puppy followed. He'd had the best of intentions when he'd resurrected the puppy, but now he was wondering what to do with him. The puppy seemed content to follow him, so for the moment, he would let it do so.

Jetrel wanted to run for the church, but the puppy wouldn't be able to keep up. Plus he was too exhausted after the resurrection. He knew that Raiel would be heading there, but all he could do now was stagger onward and pray that he made it in time.

Pray? Less than a week before, he would never have been able to comprehend the thought of himself praying. It was really amazing the transformation he had made and how quickly he had made it. Raiel, on the other hand, had changed for the worse. Now he was left wondering what would happen to them both when this whole thing was finished. He didn't think that Raiel would be allowed back into Heaven, and he didn't think he would be allowed back into Hell—not unless he was stripped of any sort of power and tossed into the lake of fire with the rest of the lost souls, but he doubted he would get off that easily. More than likely, Lucifer would find a much more severe form of torment to subject him to. He shivered at the thought despite the fact that he was sweating.

As Jetrel neared the church, he noticed that Father Stephens' car was parked outside, and he saw Raiel walking around to the side of the building. He was about to yell at Raiel, when he saw him throw a large brick through one of the stained glass windows. The glass shattered and Raiel leapt through the gaping hole where the window had been.

Jetrel started running toward the window, but stopped short when he neared the father's car. He ran to the driver's door and found it unlocked. He got inside and put the puppy on the seat next to him. Jetrel yanked the large metal cross from the rearview mirror, burning his hand and pulling the mirror from the glass as he did, and used it to punch a hole in the car's steering column. He yanked out the wires and tried to remember which two Sam had tapped together to start the other car. He couldn't remember for sure, so he ended up randomly trying wires until he managed to spark the car to life.

Jetrel gunned the engine to stop it from sputtering, snapped on his seatbelt, and dropped the car into gear. He had watched Sam closely when he was driving and hoped that he could manage to do it. The tires squeaked briefly as the car sprung forward, and Jetrel cranked the wheel toward the front doors of the church, trying to keep the vehicle on course. The puppy dropped to its belly and its legs splayed as it tried to keep from sliding into the passenger door. Jetrel grinned wickedly as some of the darkness inside him surfaced, driven by adrenaline and the wanton destruction he was about to cause. He had found goodness, but thousands of years of darkness couldn't be wiped out in a week. Jetrel supposed that he could be forgiven his occasional impulses.

The car roared toward the large double doors, bearing down on them quickly. Jetrel reached over, grabbed the puppy from the passenger seat, and hugged it to him, trying to protect it the best he could. The car slammed against the doors and nearly stopped against the heavy oak, but the doors splintered apart reluctantly, and the car burst into the church.

The car jerked once as the engine died, and Jetrel finally allowed himself to open his eyes and look around. Through the cracked windshield, he saw Lydia laying on the floor and Raiel lying nearby. The stone box was lying between them, and Raiel was already crawling toward it.

Jetrel set the puppy down beside him and undid his seatbelt. He climbed out cautiously, trying to avoid the broken boards sticking up all around him. He ran at Raiel, who had already managed to get a hold of the box, but Raiel had found a broken piece of wood and swung it at Jetrel, knocking him aside. Jetrel stumbled and tried to recover, but Raiel hit him across the back, dropping him to his knees. Jetrel rolled to the side, expecting another strike, but Raiel was stumbling toward the broken front doors. He started to stand, intending to follow, when he heard Lydia moan.

Jetrel ran over to her, touching her arm lightly as he neared. Lydia swung blindly at him, wincing in pain.

"It's okay; it's me," Jetrel said.

Lydia calmed down but didn't look at him. She continued to lie on the ground, clutching her side. Jetrel looked around and saw Father Stephens laying a short distance away near the broken stained glass window. Jetrel moved over to him, checking to make sure he was still alive. Father Stephens was breathing and appeared to be fine, with the exception of some swelling around his eye.

Jetrel turned back to the front of the church as the puppy began to bark. The puppy had somehow climbed out of the car and was watching Raiel as he returned to the church. Raiel stopped behind the car and stared in at them. He no longer had the box and was instead holding a gold lighter. He smiled at Jetrel before flipping the lid back on the lighter and snapping his thumb across the flint. The flame jumped to life, and Raiel tossed the lighter into the church. He then turned and staggered away.

Jetrel knew what was happening even before Raiel had a chance to strike the lighter's flint. He hadn't realized it before because of the dust and his own adrenaline, but the whole church had begun to smell of gasoline. As the flame touched the floor, the gasoline ignited. The floor all around the car burst into flames, bathing the church in a bright orange glow. The front entrance was now surrounded by fire, leaving only the back entrance or the broken window as the only means of escape. The window was edged in colorful shards of glass that seemed to be daring him to try to cross unscathed. Instead, he bent down, wrestled Father Stephens' unconscious body over his shoulder, and headed toward the back of the church with the puppy in tow.

Jetrel reached the back door unscathed and managed to open it and carry Father Stephens outside. He got as far from the burning church as he could before he set Father Stephens down in the grass, lowering the old priest to the ground as gently as he could. He was relieved to see that he was starting to wake up. Jetrel looked around, searching for some sign of Raiel, but he saw none. He really hated to leave the father out there unattended, but he had to go back to get Lydia. He stood up and ran back into the church, pushing the puppy back with his foot as he slipped through the door.

Jetrel ran hunched over, trying to avoid as much of the billowing smoke as he could. He went to Lydia and gently lifted her into his arms. He tried to be gentle to avoid putting pressure on her ribs, but she let out a sharp cry anyway. He ignored it and headed toward the back door again, this time not able to crouch to avoid the smoke.

Once outside, Jetrel walked over to Father Stephens, who was now sitting up and watching him carry Lydia. He set Lydia down as carefully as he could, telling Father Stephens about her ribs.

"Okay, I'll try to help her and watch over her as best I can," Father Stephens said. "What are you going to do?"

"I'm going to go after Raiel and get the box back before he does something stupid with it."

"May God go with you."

"I certainly hope he does." Jetrel turned to leave, but stopped and picked up the puppy. He handed him to Father Stephens and smiled. "Keep an eye on him, please. The last thing I need is for him to get killed. I don't think I've got the energy to deal with that again."

Father Stephens smiled, but his confusion showed. Regardless, he took the puppy and held it to his chest as Jetrel ran to the front of the church.

CHAPTER - 35 INFERNO

Jetrel reached the front of the church and saw Raiel kneeling in the grass. The box sat on the ground, and Raiel was trying desperately to open it. He turned it over repeatedly, speaking holy words in hopes that one of them would activate the box. His attention was devoted completely to the box, and he failed to notice Jetrel as he approached.

"Perhaps it only opens for those who are worthy," Jetrel said.

Raiel turned at the sound of Jetrel's voice and stood. He grabbed the box and tucked it beneath his arm.

"It doesn't matter whether you consider me worthy or not. The box will open for anyone. They simply have to figure out how to do it."

"That's where you're running into the problem, isn't it? Figuring things out has never been your strong point. It involves too much thinking."

"Mock me if you wish," Raiel said. "I have the box, and if you want it, you'll have to go through me to get it."

Jetrel leapt at the crazed angel. Raiel slid out of the way easily and dropped the box. He didn't need to worry about it right now. Jetrel wasn't going to get away with it unless he could defeat him, and that wouldn't happen.

Raiel followed Jetrel, kicking him in the back before he could regain his footing. Jetrel stumbled and fell, landing heavily on his chest. He rolled onto his back, trying to ignore the fact that he couldn't breathe. Raiel slammed his foot onto the ground, narrowly missing Jetrel as he rolled out of the way. Raiel was determined to finish him off as quickly as possible. Ordinarily, an angel would be reluctant to kill, leaving it as a last resort. Raiel's willingness to kill only managed to show how far over the edge he had truly gone.

Jetrel pushed himself up, noticing how much effort it actually took to do so. Resurrecting the puppy had taken too much out of him, and now he was facing a strong opponent who was not only at full strength, but also insane. Insanity was a dangerous weapon, and Raiel wielded it expertly.

"You look worn-out," Raiel said. "Have you been busy here on Earth? Evil must be very tiring."

"Actually, goodness is what's tiring," Jetrel said, as he regained his breath. "But you wouldn't know about that anymore."

Raiel moved fast, managing to strike Jetrel across the jaw before he noticed that the angel was in motion. Jetrel spun and dropped to the ground, his vision obscured by golden fireworks. He knew Raiel would be on top of him in an instant, but was too dazed to make his body function properly. He reached out for the only thing he could find—the stone box. He rolled to his back and thrust the box out in front of him. Raiel was in mid-swing and struck the stone box with his fist. The angel screamed and Jetrel heard a loud crack. Raiel stumbled back, holding his injured hand against his chest. Jetrel tried to stand, but Raiel leapt onto the box. Jetrel pushed back against the box, but couldn't support the angel's weight.

The stone box pressed down against Jetrel's chest and the runes lit up. A beautiful hum came from the box, drawing Raiel into a heavy trance and causing Jetrel intense pain. Jetrel screamed as the sound drove daggers of pain into his head. He rolled to the side, pushing the box and Raiel away from him. The box fell silent and the runes vanished. Raiel looked at Jetrel in disbelief.

"How did you do that?" Raiel asked.

"I don't know," Jetrel said. He looked down at the cross hanging around his neck. Raiel also noticed the cross and lunged to grab it. Jetrel rolled out of the way, grabbed the box, and pulled it to his chest. The runes lit up and pain shot through his head again. He pulled the lid from the box as quickly as he could and tossed it to the ground. He held the box away from his chest and the sound stopped. Raiel grabbed it and both angels looked inside. There was nothing inside but a silk pillow. Raiel yanked the box away and began feeling around inside it as if the key might have somehow become invisible.

"What did you do with it?" Raiel asked.

"What could I have done with it? You've been with me the whole time and you saw me open it."

Raiel threw the box aside. He stared at Jetrel in disbelief before turning back toward the church. Jetrel immediately grasped what Raiel was thinking as he started running for the front door of the church.

Jetrel started to shout his protest, but it was cut short as the flames hit the car's gas tank and it exploded. Jetrel shielded his face, but Raiel was knocked over backwards. He quickly stood and continued toward the church. Jetrel watched Raiel go in and then did the only thing he could; he followed him into the inferno.

The intense heat stopped Jetrel like a wall. He held his breath and then pushed his way into the church. He had dealt with flames and heat on a daily basis in Hell, but this situation was different. In Hell, he could endure the flames and come out intact, but here his body wouldn't be able to survive.

The flames had spread throughout the entire building. Jetrel saw Raiel at the front of the church, throwing chairs and tipping pews in search of the key. Jetrel ran after him through the flames, gritting his teeth as his skin blistered. Raiel kicked the altar over, too busy searching to notice Jetrel running at him.

Jetrel leapt at Raiel, driving him to the floor. Raiel pushed him off and got up to resume his search.

"Just let it burn," Jetrel said. "Then no one will be able to have it."

"I can't do that. I need it to get back into Heaven. I have to find it."

"In other words, you don't care about the mission anymore. You only care about saving yourself."

Raiel swung a broken chair leg, hitting Jetrel on the side of the head. Jetrel didn't have time to register what had happened before darkness overwhelmed him and he fell to the ground. Raiel climbed uneasily to his feet. He needed to find the key, but the smoke was choking him. He found that he had little choice but to leave before the smoke and flames consumed him. He didn't know whether or not the key could be destroyed by fire, but if he died in there, he would never get the chance to find out. At least, by killing Jetrel, the flames would finally accomplish what he couldn't.

CHAPTER - 36 LYDIA

Lydia knew she had to get up. She could feel the grass beneath her, so she knew she wasn't in the church anymore. She rolled over slowly, trying not to move her chest. The pain in her ribs was intense—easily the worst pain she'd ever experienced. She had heard that childbirth was the worst pain a woman could endure, but at the moment, she had a hard time believing that.

When she felt that she could sit up without passing out, she did so slowly. She looked over at Father Stephens, as he clutched a small puppy and stared blankly at the burning church in front of him. He appeared to be in shock and didn't notice as Lydia struggled to stand.

"Where are you going?" Father Stephens asked when he finally noticed her.

"I've got to go get the key," Lydia said.

"Why? Just let the flames consume it. The world would be better off without it."

"We don't even know if fire can destroy it, much less what would happen if it did. Besides, I don't think it's our decision to make. I think we should let God decide what to do with the key."

Father Stephens clutched the puppy to his chest and sighed. He looked beyond tired and in no condition to enter the church again. Lydia wasn't in any better shape, but one of them had to try to get the key back. She started toward the church, expecting an argument from Father Stephens, but she received none. As she walked, her legs seemed to steady themselves, and as long as she breathed shallowly, her ribs didn't hurt too much.

Lydia entered the back door of the church where the flames weren't as intense. She made her way toward the altar, covering her nose and mouth with her shirt as she went. The smoke was building, so she wanted to find the key and get out as quickly as possible.

She heard Jetrel moan before she saw him, but knew it was him immediately. She headed toward the sound, maneuvering around the broken pews, chairs, and the altar. She struggled to see through the heavy smoke and nearly fell several times before reaching him. She knelt next to him and shook him gently. He moaned again and stirred slightly. She shouted at him to get up and slapped him several times across the face. Jetrel woke up, blinking a few times to make his eyes regain their focus. He looked up at Lydia in disbelief.

"What are you doing in here?" Jetrel asked. "You're hurt."

"If I hadn't come in here, you would have died, then where would we be?"

"Did Raiel get the key?"

"No, it's still hidden. You wait here. I'll get it."

Lydia crawled across the floor, trying to avoid the smoke. She began throwing debris aside, careful to avoid her injured ribs. She searched until she found the key. It lay among the flowers and the broken vase in which she had hidden it. She grabbed it and turned back to Jetrel, fighting the urges that the key was putting in her head.

"Okay, now let's get out of here. Can you move?"

"I think so," Jetrel said.

Lydia crawled over to him and helped him up as best she could. Jetrel got to his feet and followed Lydia as she threaded her way through the smoke and debris. She walked to the door, stumbling and coughing. She shoved the door open and took a deep breath of fresh air. Jetrel followed right behind her and they both collapsed onto the grass. Father Stephens ran up to them and helped them crawl away from the burning building.

"Are you two alright?" Father Stephens asked.

"I think so," Jetrel said.

"We've got to get out of here," Father Stephens said. He set the puppy down and got to his feet. "Raiel's nearby and he's been looking for you two. He keeps circling the church."

"Okay," Lydia said. "Let's go, Jetrel." She stood up, took Jetrel's arm, and helped him to stand again. She gasped as Raiel stepped around the side of the church, smiling eerily. It was the look of a man not entirely in his right mind. If there were a more terrifying look that a person could have on his face, none of them would want to see it.

"You've deceived me, you've fought me, and you've hindered me every step of the way," Raiel said. "I've tried to take it all in stride and be the bigger person, but that's all over with now. I'm done with your games and your lies."

Raiel lifted a tire iron and rested it on his shoulder. He started toward them, when Father Stephens charged at him. Raiel stopped in surprise and was knocked over backwards by the old priest. Jetrel saw his chance and grabbed Lydia's arm as she tried to run to help Father Stephens.

"We need to get out of here," Jetrel said. "Father Stephens bought us some time, now we need to use it."

Lydia hesitantly allowed herself to be dragged away, but her gaze stayed on the two men wrestling on the church lawn. Jetrel grabbed the puppy and ran as quickly as he could, which wouldn't have been considered quick by anyone's standards. He pulled Lydia into an alley nearby and collapsed behind a dumpster.

"Where are we going to go?" Lydia asked. "We can't stay here for long."

"I know," Jetrel said. "Raiel's probably following us, and if he isn't, he will be soon. We have to find a place to hide until we can figure out what to do with the key."

"We have to hurry. The key's starting to take over my thoughts, and I don't think I can fight it for much longer. If we don't hurry, it's going to make me go back to the church and open the gate of the Abyss. Maybe you should take it for a while."

"I can't take it," Jetrel said. "I can be summoned back to Hell at any time. If I take the key, then I can be summoned back, and the demons can take it from me by force. We've just gotta get somewhere safe."

"I know where we can go," Lydia said. "Hurry, we need to keep moving."

Lydia stood up and started running down the alley. Jetrel stood and followed her, watching behind him in case

Raiel was following them. He was worried about Father Stephens, but if he went back to find out what happened to him, the priest's sacrifice would have been for nothing. All he could do now was follow Lydia and hope for the best.

CHAPTER - 37 FATHER STEPHENS

Father Stephens watched Raiel from the moment he emerged from behind the church. He was carrying a tire iron and had the look of a madman, watching Jetrel and Lydia as he approached, not seeming to notice the priest. Father Stephens looked to the bloodied and beaten pair that held Raiel's focus. They were in no condition to defend themselves and would be able to do little to protect the key. Anger rose in the aging priest as Raiel approached, and he used it to buy Jetrel and Lydia some time.

Now Father Stephens found himself fighting with Raiel, doing anything he could to keep the angel from pursuing the key. Even a few seconds might be enough to prevent him from catching up to Jetrel and Lydia. Raiel was struggling to free himself, with little success. Father Stephens was grabbing at Raiel's clothes, hair, and anything else he could get a hold of to keep Raiel on the ground.

Raiel grabbed Father Stephens' arms and tried to push him off, but he bit Raiel's shirt and held on. Raiel punched Father Stephens, finally freeing himself. Father Stephens rolled away and got up. He planned to attack Raiel again, but the adrenaline had started to wear off, and his body felt rubbery and heavy.

"What did you do that for?" Raiel asked.

"To keep you from the key," Father Stephens said. "You've lost your mind and can't be trusted with it."

"We've been over this," Raiel said.

Raiel walked over to Father Stephens, lifting the tire iron over his head. Father Stephens stared up at it, not bothering to try to block the blow. Raiel stopped, poised to strike. He hesitated for a moment before lowering the weapon. He stared a moment longer before turning and running in the direction in which he had last seen Jetrel and Lydia go.

Father Stephens wanted to try to follow Raiel, but something else grabbed his attention. Lying in the grass near the church was the stone box that the key of the Abyss had been in, and next to it was a book. It lay open, its pages flapping in the breeze. Father Stephens got up and walked over to the book. He picked it up and tucked it into the waist of his pants as he walked away from the burning church. He heard the wailing of fire engines growing louder as they approached, and then a wave of vertigo hit him. He tried to sit down, but ended up falling face-first onto the grass.

Then the sirens were gone, and he saw Jetrel and Raiel battling above a lush green field. The two angels fought furiously, but Raiel was stronger and faster than Jetrel. The battle was over quickly as Raiel dove in close to Jetrel and grabbed his wings. He took hold of Jetrel's wings near the base, planted his foot in the middle of his back, and began to pull. Jetrel screamed like a siren as Raiel tore the wings off his back and then watched him tumble toward the ground below. Jetrel landed with a soft thud, and Raiel dropped from the sky after him. He landed heavily on Jetrel's body, humiliating his opponent even more. He stood on Jetrel's broken body for a moment before reaching down and tearing the necklace from around Jetrel's neck. Instead of the crucifix that Father Stephens remembers hanging there, he saw the key of the Abyss.

Raiel gripped the key tightly and stepped off Jetrel's body. He walked over to the portal that glowed amongst the burnt remnants of the church. He drove the key into the ground and turned it. A huge crack appeared in the Earth beneath him, and demonic figures began to emerge. Raiel laughed and his features twisted into an evil visage of their former selves.

Father Stephens awoke screaming. He stopped himself as he realized that it had simply been another vision. He looked around and saw that he was in the back of an ambulance. The EMT was trying to calm him down, while another one was treating his wounds. Father Stephens relaxed a little, letting the men do their jobs. His head was pounding, but that was the least of his concerns. He had just witnessed Jetrel lose the battle for the key. Raiel had acted just as they all thought he would. The evil in his heart had consumed him, and he'd used the key to doom humanity instead of returning it to Heaven. He didn't know what he could do to help Jetrel when the final battle started, but he knew that he had to find him and warn him about what he had witnessed. It might not change the outcome, but he had to try.

CHAPTER - 38 LYDIA

Lydia moved as quickly as her injuries would allow. Jetrel kept up easily, despite his own injuries. Lydia frequently looked over her shoulder, expecting to see Raiel, but luckily they seemed to have lost him.

Lydia navigated her way through the back alleys of the city with the ease of experience, until she came upon a familiar sight. She ran to the back door of the strip club and collapsed against the door. She was breathing heavily, and with every breath, the pain in her ribs got worse. As the adrenaline started to wear off, her pain began to grow.

Jetrel looked up at the sign above the door and smiled. "Eden's Shadow, huh?"

"Yeah," Lydia said. "Why's that funny?"

"Not funny—ironic," Jetrel said. "Earth's been in Eden's shadow since Adam and Eve were thrown out. That's part of the reason Lucifer rebelled."

"Because they ate an apple and were thrown out of the Garden of Eden?"

"It's not about what they ate or didn't eat. It's about following the word of God. When they failed to do so, Lucifer claimed that they were unworthy of God's adoration and that they should be destroyed. God refused and so started Lucifer's resentment of humanity."

"If we don't hurry and get inside, then Raiel may help Lucifer fulfill his desire to destroy us," Lydia said. Jetrel knelt beside her and helped her get to her feet. She leaned heavily against him as she dug through her pocket for the keys. She found them and managed to get the door open. Jetrel helped her through the door, where she was met by several of her coworkers getting ready to go out on stage.

"What happened to you?" one of the women asked. Lydia looked up at the woman, a pale redhead named Rena. It was Rena who had asked the question, but she was followed closely by Selene and Rashel. Selene was a short Mexican woman, and Rashel was black with beautiful long hair. Lydia didn't know either of them very well, but Rena had always been a good friend. The three women came over and helped Lydia and Jetrel into one of the dressing rooms and onto the couch.

"We were attacked," Lydia said. "Jetrel tried to help me, but there were too many of them. We just barely managed to get away."

"Oh my God!" Rashel said. "We better call the cops and get you guys an ambulance."

"No," Lydia said. "We'll be fine. Besides you know that Mike hates having the cops out here. We just need someplace to rest until we can be sure the guys who attacked us are gone."

"You should really call the cops," Selene said. "Who cares what Mike thinks about having cops in his club? It would be better to have the cops catch these guys than to let them stay out there to attack someone else."

"Please," Jetrel said. "Don't call the cops. I've got a warrant out for my arrest. If you call them, then they'll just haul me away and maybe Lydia too since she's been helping me hide out. I couldn't stand to see her take the fall for helping me."

The girls looked at each other before turning back to Lydia.

"No problem," Selene said. "You can just hide out here for a while. Mike doesn't come back here, so no one should bother you. If you guys need anything, just let us know. Do you need something for your puppy?"

Jetrel looked down at the puppy in his arms. He had been so quiet that Jetrel hadn't even realized he'd still been holding him.

"Yeah," Jetrel said. "If you have some water and anything he can eat, that would be great."

"Okay," Rena said. "I'll run over to the corner store across the street and pick up some dog food and a couple bowls. I'll get you guys something to eat and drink too."

"Thank you," Lydia said. She smiled at the women, who smiled back before leaving the room and shutting the door behind them. Jetrel and Lydia rested on the couch for a while before Rena returned. There were several more women with her. They all made a big deal about the puppy, and they all played with him. Rena set up the food and water bowls, and the puppy ate and drank ravenously. Finally, Rena motioned for Lydia and Jetrel to follow her. They both got up and followed her into the hall.

"I'm going to let you two hang out in another dressing room," Rena said. "That way, you can have some privacy, 'cause as long as that puppy's in that room, the girls will be in there too."

"Thanks again," Lydia said. She hugged Rena briefly before turning to go into the dressing room.

"Will the puppy be okay?" Jetrel asked. "I don't want him to have an accident or anything."

"He'll be fine," Rena said. "He's in good hands. The only problem may be getting him back from the girls when you're ready to go." Rena laughed. Jetrel smiled at her before following Lydia into the dressing room.

"Are you okay?" Jetrel asked once they were inside.

"I'll be fine," Lydia said. "The pain is starting to set in, though."

"I know. It seems like all I've known is pain since I arrived on Earth. Everywhere I go, someone seems to beat me up."

Lydia had sat down on the couch and was staring at the key in her hand. She hadn't heard Jetrel's last comment. She was becoming more and more obsessed with the key. Now that the adrenaline had worn off, she could hear the key's voice in her head again. It was trying to lure her into going back to the church to open the portal and unleash the plagues. She was about to get up when the key vanished from her sight. She shook her head, looked again, and saw that there was a towel covering the key. She looked up at Jetrel, who was standing in front of her.

"It's getting to you, isn't it? The key's a powerful artifact, one that humans were never meant to possess."

"I'm sorry," Lydia said. "The urge to use it is nearly overwhelming. While we were running from Raiel, I couldn't hear its voice, but now that it's quiet, it seems to be speaking to me."

"I know," Jetrel said. "It's the same voice I heard in my mind guiding me to it. You need to hide it somewhere. Once it's no longer in contact with you, the voice will disappear."

"Won't Raiel be able to track the key back here and find us?" Lydia asked. She walked over to the linen cabinet, set the key inside, and covered it with towels.

"In his current state of mind? I doubt it. You need to be able to relax and concentrate to follow the key's voice. Raiel is filled with so much anger and hatred right now that I doubt he would be able to relax his mind enough."

"I hope you're right."

Lydia walked back to the couch and sat down. Jetrel walked over, sat beside her, and put his arm around her. She laid her head against his chest and they sat in silence, each trying to decide what to do next.

CHAPTER - 39 RAIEL

Raiel ran from the church, barely escaping before the police and fire trucks arrived. He had to find Lydia before she gave the key to Jetrel and he returned to Hell. If that happened, then Raiel might be following shortly after. He had screwed up everything he'd tried to do on Earth, and he had no options left. Returning the key to Heaven was the only hope he had of redeeming himself.

Raiel ran down the alley where he last saw Jetrel and Lydia. Once he rounded the corner, though, he had no idea where to go. There was no trail to follow and many directions they could have taken. If they were smart, they would be weaving randomly through alleys and streets, until they finally found a place to hide. In a city this big, he would never be able to find them.

"Damn it, old man," Raiel said. He debated going back to question Father Stephens, but he wouldn't be able to get near him with all the cops and firefighters around. The old priest screwed everything up, and now Raiel's mission was on the verge of failing. He wished he'd killed the priest when he'd had the chance.

Raiel started walking the streets randomly, hoping to find some sort of clue. It was a long shot, but there was little else to do. He tried several times to sense the key, but his mind was a wreck. There were too many things happening too quickly, and he doubted his own perceptions.

Finally, with little else to do, Raiel gave up. He needed to rest and try to come up with a plan. The church was burning down, and Lydia's apartment was probably being watched by the cops. Even if it wasn't, he didn't want to be found there sleeping if Jetrel and Lydia decided to go there.

After several minutes, Raiel decided to head back to the abandoned clothing store where he had first tracked the key. He would probably be able to find a safe spot to rest without being bothered. There would be bums coming in and out, but he hoped that if he left them alone, they would do the same for him.

After several attempts, Raiel managed to find the right building. He lifted the window and slithered inside. It was daytime, so the place was deserted. All the bums were probably out scrounging through dumpsters or begging people for money. That whole lifestyle disgusted him.

Raiel managed to find a discreet place that wasn't soaked in urine. He sat down and tried to calm himself enough to track the key, but it wasn't working. He swore loudly before lying down and trying to get some sleep.

Raiel slipped into sleep quickly, his dreams haunted by images of fire and torment. He slept heavily for several hours before being awoken by noises in the store. He jerked awake and sat up quickly. There were several bums in the building staking out their campsites. They were watching Raiel as he scanned the room, but quickly forgot his presence and returned to their preparations.

Raiel saw that the light in the room had dimmed significantly, which meant it was late in the evening. He debated going out and searching for the key again, but dismissed it. There was little hope of finding them that way. If

Jetrel was planning on using the key, he would have done so by now. The fire at the church should be out by now, so there should have been no reason for Jetrel not to open the portal. That meant that Lydia hadn't given him the key, or he really wasn't planning on using it or returning it to Hell.

Raiel leaned back against the wall and watched the humans in front of him. They were disgusting creatures that he was starting to hate more and more with every passing second.

Humans' lives seemed to be enveloped in pain. The atrocities they didn't do to each other, they did to themselves. Their whole society was created out of war and turmoil. What they didn't have, they went out and took by force, no matter how much it hurt anyone else. It was a trend that seemed to get worse every year. The more civilized they supposedly became, the easier it was for them to hurt others. It seemed to be an innate defect in their makeup.

Raiel sighed as his thoughts began to speed up and grow darker.

God told the angels to bow before his greatest creation, which nearly all of them had done. The only one to stand up and say no had been Lucifer. He'd been the greatest of God's angels and the only one who wouldn't subjugate himself to the humans. The angels were created first and had done God's bidding faithfully and without question ever since. Then humans came along, and the angels were tossed aside while God played with his new toys. Lucifer was the only one to speak up for their rights.

It was a dark time for the angels, and one for which Raiel hadn't been around. He was one of the youngest archangels, but he wondered which side he would have chosen had he been there for the battle. Before leaving Heaven, he would have taken God's side without hesitation, but after dealing with humanity firsthand, he wasn't so sure. He was beginning to understand why Lucifer did what he did and to sympathize with him. He hadn't been defying God out of hatred; he'd simply been trying to stop an injustice from occurring.

Raiel leaned forward as an idea occurred to him. Why did he need to get the key and return it to Heaven? If he did, he would be facing discipline, or worse, at the hands of God. He had taken the lives of some of God's pets and, for that, he would suffer. If he took the key and delivered it to Lucifer or opened the gate of the Abyss, he would probably be welcomed as a hero. He would be the second angel to strike back at God and take a stand for his kind. He wouldn't bow to these humans as God commanded. He would become a martyr like Lucifer, and then together they would fight to restore the angels to their former glory.

Raiel smiled. It was a twisted monstrosity that warped his face into an evil visage. He would be through worrying about what God would do to him and would instead turn his attention to destroying the vermin God loved so much.

"What the Hell are you staring at?" one of the bums asked him. "You've been watching us all evening and it's giving me the creeps."

"Besides, this is our home," another one said. "Who said you could come in here and set up camp?"

"No one," Raiel said. "I don't take orders from anyone. Not anymore." Raiel picked up the tire iron and walked toward the five men, smiling as he went.

"What are you doing?" one of them asked. "Don't do anything stupid. There are five of us and only one of you. I wouldn't want you to get hurt."

"Don't worry, I won't," Raiel said.

The screaming inside of the old clothing store seemed to go on forever. Had there been anyone outside, they would have almost certainly called the cops. Luckily for Raiel, this neighborhood had little foot traffic.

CHAPTER - 40 JETREL

Jetrel woke with Rena standing over him, shaking him gently. He looked around and saw that he and Lydia had fallen asleep on the sofa. Lydia was still asleep, her head resting on his chest. He ran his hand through her hair and she opened her eyes. She looked up at Jetrel first, then at Rena.

"What's wrong?" Lydia asked.

"Nothing," Rena said. "It's closing time. Do you guys have somewhere to stay?"

"No," Jetrel said. "We hadn't really thought that far ahead."

"Do you think we could stay here?" Lydia asked. "I don't really feel safe going back out there tonight."

"That shouldn't be a problem," Rena said. "You'll just have to hide until after Mike walks the building. You know how he is. He checks every room before he locks up for the night. You two should be able to pull the sofa out enough to get behind it. Just pull it back as close to the wall as you can once you're back there. He shouldn't notice anything out of the ordinary."

"Thanks, Rena," Lydia said. Rena smiled at them before leaving the room. Jetrel and Lydia got up slowly, each careful not to jostle their wounded bodies too much. They pulled the couch from against the wall and got behind it. They pulled it as close to the wall as they could and waited. It took about twenty minutes before Mike entered the room. Jetrel and Lydia held their breath and waited as he walked around the room. The footsteps stopped once for several seconds, but then they heard him leave the room, pulling the door shut behind him.

Jetrel and Lydia slid the couch forward and stepped out from behind it. They were starting to push it back into place, when they heard voices in the hall. They debated getting back behind the couch, but there wasn't time as they heard someone approaching.

"Just a second!" a voice yelled from the hall. "I've gotta get my bra!"

The door opened and Selene walked in. She quickly walked over to Lydia and pulled the puppy from her oversized purse. She handed it to her and smiled. She turned back to the door and grabbed a bra that was draped over the back of the makeup chair before leaving the room.

"There! Did that take so long?" Selene yelled, as she slammed the door shut behind her.

Jetrel and Lydia sat on the sofa in silence until enough time had passed that they felt safe leaving the room. Lydia went to get the food that Rena had picked up for them, while Jetrel walked out onto the empty stage. He looked down at the tables below and imagined them full of gawking, horny men. He didn't know how Lydia could stand in front of them and take her clothes off every day. It must be a very bizarre experience.

Lydia came out carrying the bags of food in one hand and the puppy's food and water balanced in the other. She walked down the stairs and began to set up the food and drinks on one of the tables. Jetrel followed her and sat down. Once Lydia was done, they ate quietly. The selection of food wasn't the best, but it was better than nothing. It consisted of a lot of junk food and pop. They both ate quickly, until the food was gone. Then they sat quietly for a while, content to watch the puppy explore the room. Finally, Jetrel felt compelled to break the silence.

"How long have you worked here?"

"A little over two years," Lydia said.

"Why did you start dancing?"

"I found out that a friend of mine in college, Sara, was a dancer. She told me that the club was looking for another girl and that I should go audition. I told her she was crazy, but she was persistent. She kept telling me about how much money she was making and how easy it was. I kept turning her down, but eventually the thought of the money got to me. I was having trouble making it financially, going to school full-time and working part-time as a store clerk. Finally, I told her I would go check it out." Lydia got up and walked over to the stage. She hopped onto the stage and sat down, her legs dangling over the edge. She seemed to be uncomfortable with the conversation, but Jetrel wasn't about to let it go. He got up, went to the stage, and leaned against it, waiting for Lydia to continue.

"At the audition, I was really nervous, but I got on stage and started the routine that Sara had helped me learn. At first, I was pretty stiff, but as the routine went on, I loosened up and got into it. When I was done, the manager told me that I was hired."

"How was it the first night on stage in front of a crowd?"

"Terrifying," Lydia said. Her legs were swinging, her heels thumping lightly against the wall. "It took me several days of performing before I began to loosen up. Finally, I began to relax and stopped paying attention to the audience. After that, I started making a lot more money and finally began to get caught up on my bills. It's not exactly the job I would have chosen, but it's helped me out a lot in my life."

"When this is all over, are you going to go back to dancing?"

"I don't know. I'd like to, but I don't think I could handle it. After nearly being raped in that alley, and then again in my apartment, I don't think I could ever look at the men in the audience the same way. I would only see them as potential attackers. I think that when this is all over, my dancing career will be too."

"It could be worse," Jetrel said. "When this is all over for me, the only thing I have to look forward to is an eternity in Hell."

"Isn't there any way that you can stay on Earth?"

"Not for long. If Raiel doesn't kill me to get the key, then Lucifer will send someone else to do it. He doesn't look too kindly on deserters."

"What does Lucifer want with the key anyway? Father Stephens and I were discussing it while we were driving around, and we couldn't figure out why he would go to all this trouble to get it. All it would do is torment humanity for a few months and then it would be over."

"The plagues contained within the Abyss are contained within a chamber beneath the Earth. When the gate is opened, the plagues will be released. Lucifer has known for centuries that the key of the Abyss was on Earth. Rumors of the key being lost have been swirling around since it was ripped from

Michael's belt. Demons spend most of their time hidden within the shadows, and angels often travel to Earth to help keep the humans from destroying themselves. Angels have a tendency to gossip with one another when they get together. They're a lot like humans in that way. It was only a matter of time before a demon would overhear the rumor. They love to stalk angels.

When Lucifer found out that the key had been lost, he sent his minions to begin searching for the Abyss. When they finally found it, they made their way into the chamber from beneath. The abyss is warded to keep things from getting out, but not to keep things from getting in. The demons entered the chamber until it was filled, but none of them can leave until the gate is opened. Once someone opens the gate, the demons will emerge to wipe out humanity."

"Why wouldn't Lucifer do that anyway? Even if it was an angel that opened the gate, his demons would still be able to escape onto Earth."

"The gate would be opened during the Apocalypse when Hell and Heaven would be preparing for the final battle. Satan would want all his minions preparing for battle. He wouldn't want to waste them by having them ravage the Earth when it was already being ravaged by the end of days. He would want their numbers for his armies."

"Would you have fought against the angels in the final battle if you hadn't been sent to Earth to find the key?"

"Yes," Jetrel said. "Before I had my eyes opened by my experiences on Earth, I would have killed as many angels as I could and reveled in the sight of their blood. So many years in Hell fueled my hatred. When you're immersed in flames and torment for so long, hatred is the only thing you have left to hang onto."

"Are you scared to be taken back to Hell?"

"Yes," Jetrel said. "I know that when I go back, I won't be welcomed with open arms. I know that Lucifer will be furious, but what scares me even more is that I may fail to protect the key. If I can save humanity, at least I will have that memory to focus on during my torment. It would help to know that no matter how much torture Lucifer put me through, it was I who destroyed his plans. I think that knowledge would help me to get through the rest of eternity."

"I wish there was something I could do to help you," Lydia said. "I can't believe that there's no way to save you. You've changed, and it doesn't seem right to punish you for what you did in your past. People can change."

"The problem is that I'm not a person; I'm an angel, and a fallen one at that. God cast me out, and no matter what I do, I cannot be allowed back into Heaven. Even if there were a way, the other angels wouldn't tolerate one of the fallen being back within their midst. I won't be accepted anywhere now."

Lydia sat in silence, not knowing what else to say. Finally, she got up, walked over to Jetrel, and wrapped her arms around him. She laid her head on his chest, listening to the sound of his heartbeat. Jetrel hesitated a moment before returning her embrace. They stood like that for several minutes before Lydia looked up at Jetrel. She smiled at him before standing on her tiptoes to kiss him. Jetrel started to pull back, but his desire got the best of him and he leaned into her kiss. It was passionate and meaningful, which was something Jetrel hadn't known a kiss could be.

Jetrel picked Lydia up and set her on the edge of the stage. Her face was now on the same level as his, which made kissing easier. Lydia reached down and pulled Jetrel's shirt over his head. Jetrel began to unbutton Lydia's shirt slowly, when she stopped him. She took him by the hand and led him back to the dressing room. The puppy followed behind them, but was shooed back into the hall, and the door was shut behind them.

CHAPTER 41 - FATHER STEPHENS

Father Stephens woke as the puppy was shooed out of the dressing room and the door closed. He had just witnessed the exchange between them in one of his visions. He felt like a voyeur eavesdropping on their private conversation, but it had allowed him to discover their location. It would give him a chance to find them before Raiel did and warn them about the vision he had experienced of Jetrel's defeat.

Father Stephens cringed as he pulled the IV from his arm and the breathing mask from his face. He didn't think that he had inhaled that much smoke at the church, but apparently the hospital didn't want to take any chances. He pulled the rest of the electrodes and wires from his body and got out of bed.

His legs were sore from his fight with Raiel, but he would have to deal with it if he wanted to get to Jetrel and Lydia in time.

The old priest went to the small wardrobe in the room and found his clothing hanging inside with the book he'd found at the church resting on the shelf above them. His clothing had been cleaned and neatly hung up. Even his shoes had been cleaned. He grabbed everything and went to the bathroom to change.

When Father Stephens came out of the bathroom, there was a nurse and two police officers waiting for him. He contemplated shoving past them, but decided to wait and see what they had to say.

"Father Stephens," the nurse said. "What are you doing out of bed and why are you dressed? The doctor wants to keep you another day for observation. You were suffering from smoke inhalation and were pretty badly hurt. There may be some internal injuries. You need to get back into bed until we can determine that you're alright."

"I'm sorry," Father Stephens said, "but I've got somewhere to be. I appreciate the precautions you're taking, but I'll be just fine."

"Well," one of the officers said, "if you're well enough to leave, then you're well enough to answer a few questions for us."

"What kinds of questions?" Father Stephens asked.

"We were wondering about how your car ended up inside the church. It was determined that the fire started when someone lit gasoline that was leaking from the car's tank. We want to know exactly what happened."

"I really don't have time for this," Father Stephens said.

"We either do this here, or we can take you down to the station."

Father Stephens didn't waste any time trying to argue; he needed to get out of there as quickly as he could. He lunged at one of the cops, driving his elbow into the man's abdomen. He doubled over, and Father Stephens shoved the other cop aside, catching him off guard, and ran for the door. He ran down the hallway as the nurse screamed behind him. There would be people chasing him now, and his only hope was to get out of the hospital.

The old priest had hoped for a quick escape, but found himself turned around in the maze of corridors. He tried to find a sign pointing him toward the exit, but couldn't find one, so he continued running. As he was about to round a corner, he looked back and saw the two cops running toward him. He turned the corner, praying for a way out, when he saw a sign pointing toward a stairwell. He ran through the door, hoping the cops hadn't seen him. As he made his way down the stairs, he heard the door above him slam open; his hopes for a smooth getaway were crushed.

As the cops slowly closed the gap, Father Stephens saw a sign below pointing him in the direction of the parking garage. He ran through the door and continued across the parking garage, glancing back over his shoulder several times. He kept expecting to see the cops coming through the door after him, but they never did. Father Stephens said a quick thank you to God for the good fortune, because he knew he couldn't have outrun them much longer.

When Father Stephens reached the parking gate, he slipped around the yellow and black striped gate arm and took one last glance back at the door before running across the street, looking for a cab as he went.

As the old priest ran across the street, the stairwell door finally opened. Raiel stepped out, his clothing covered in blood. He wiped the blood from the tire iron, and he watched the priest stumble across the street. He needed to find the key, and he wasn't about to allow a couple of cops to screw up his only chance of finding it. Now Father Stephens would lead him to wherever Jetrel and Lydia were hiding.

Father Stephens managed to flag down a cab and climbed in the back.

"Where to?" the cabbie asked.

"Eden's Shadow, please."

The cabbie gave him an odd look before starting the meter and pulling into traffic.

Father Stephens ignored the cabbie's judgment and instead pulled the book he had found from the waistband of his pants and opened it. It was a journal, and quite an old one from the looks of it. It must have been under the pillow in the stone box. He had a little bit of time before they reached the club, so he decided to read it and see if it could provide him with any answers.

CHAPTER 42 - THE JOURNAL

I am Father Jacobs and if you're reading this, then the key of the Abyss has been found. I hope that it has been found by one of the righteous angels, but if not, then God help those who dwell upon the Earth.

I have to write quickly since my brothers are nearly ready to bury the key deep beneath the ground.

I am a member of an order called the Guardians of the Abyss. It is an ancient order created by Father Riggs to protect the secret of the key of the Abyss.

Father Riggs was told of the key through visions sent to him by the archangel Michael. The visions showed the loss of the key during the battle between the angels and how to find its resting place. Father Riggs followed the directions from the archangel, which led him to the key. After unearthing it, he wrapped it in a piece of cloth and returned with it to his church.

Over the next few months, Father Riggs kept the key a secret while he worked on carving a box for it out of stone. Michael showed Father Riggs how to create the box by sending him more visions. It was slow work, but Father Riggs kept at it diligently. When the box was completed, Michael showed Father Riggs the proper runes and incantations to carve into the stone to help keep the key locked safely inside. With the runes in place, the only way the box will open is when it comes in contact with a holy item, which will make it more difficult for the fallen to open it should it fall into their possession.

Then Father Riggs found the finest silk that he could and used it to create a pillow upon which the key could rest. Once this was done, the key was placed inside the box to remain hidden until the time that the angels came to Earth to retrieve it.

As Father Riggs worked, he began to find others in the church that he deemed trustworthy enough to tell about the key. Together, these individuals created the Guardians of the Abyss and swore an oath to do whatever they must to keep the key safe and out of the hands of the fallen. The Guardians of the Abyss safely protected the key for generations, always keeping its existence a secret.

I was asked to join the organization after many years abroad doing missionary work. I was brought into the organization at the same time as a young man called Brother Taren. He was an ambitious young man, always eager to help and full of questions. He had spent many years working for the church in his hometown and was quickly gaining attention from the higher-ups. I heard stories that he was even invited to speak with the Cardinal about his charitable works.

The members of the Guardians would often meet in the church basement to discuss matters of the church and the key. A lot of time was spent in search of the location of the gate, but with little success. We had hoped to split the members of the Guardians to watch over the key as well as the gate.

Then one day when Brother Taren was cleaning, he found a loose stone block in the basement wall. When he pulled it out, he found an old scroll hidden behind it. It was written by Father Riggs and told of the gate of the Abyss. It said that the gate was located in America and included directions on how to find it. It was an exciting discovery for all of us. We spent many hours reading and rereading the scroll and making plans to send several of us to America.

It was several days later when I awoke to screaming coming from the basement. I ran downstairs to find the bodies of several of the Guardians on the floor, and the box containing the key was missing.

The remaining members of the Guardians gathered at the church. The only member that we couldn't find was Brother Taren. Many of the members were worried that something had happened to him, but I had a feeling that there was a more sinister reason for his disappearance.

Those of us who remained decided that we should go to America to find the gate. We boarded the first boat that we could find and settled in for a long voyage.

After several long months, we arrived in America and immediately set out for the location of the gate. Finding the scroll containing the gate's location was a big discovery, and we had all read the scroll many times, so finding the location wasn't difficult.

The journey was difficult, but we persevered and reached the gate. When we arrived, we found that others had arrived ahead of us. Brother Taren and several other men were in the midst of a satanic ritual in preparation to open the gate. Upon seeing us, Brother Taren ordered his followers to attack us. It was a bloody fight, but we had nearly double their numbers and managed to slaughter them all, with the exception of Brother Taren.

Brother Taren was bound and questioned in depth. He told us that Lucifer's minions had heard whisperings of the key's presence, and that it had been found. After many years, these minions managed to find the location of the key, but didn't know where to find the gate. Brother Taren began doing work for the church in hopes that he could infiltrate the Guardians of the Abyss. Then, after finding the location of the gate, he stole the key and brought his followers to America.

Taren proudly told us everything he had done and that he regretted none of it. He was too dangerous, and he knew too much. So with little else to do, we dispatched Brother Taren and had one final meeting of the Guardians.

After much discussion, we realized that we needed to hide the key and disband the Guardians of the Abyss. There was talk of destroying the key, but it was a powerful holy artifact. To destroy it would take a powerful celestial weapon, such as an angel's sword. We had no way of finding such a weapon, so all we could do was to hide the key where no one would find it.

The remaining Guardians and I dug a deep pit several miles from the location of the gate in which to bury the box. There it should remain forgotten until such a time as the angels return for it. We also decided to build a church upon the site of the gate to help hide it from those who wish to open it. Together, we will serve at this church until our deaths. At that time, the secrets of the Guardians will die as well.

Now as we prepare to bury the box, I pray that it will lie safe and hidden from the fallen. If someone other than one of the angels finds this key, please keep it safe and hidden from those who would use it against you. May God bless you and watch over you.

In the service of God,

Father Jacobs

CHAPTER 43 - EDEN'S SHADOW

Jetrel slept on the couch in the dressing room with his arm around Lydia, and the puppy slept at their feet. Jetrel stretched and yawned as the morning sun started peeking through the dirty window. He leaned over and kissed Lydia on the cheek. Lydia stirred and turned her head to look at him.

"Good morning," Lydia said. "How did you sleep?"

"Great," Jetrel said. "How about you?"

"I slept well too. For the first time since that night in the alley, I felt safe."

"I'm glad," Jetrel said.

The puppy got up and began licking their faces. Lydia laughed and sat up, wincing as she moved her ribs. Jetrel sat up as well, faring a lot better than Lydia was.

"I'm going to go take the puppy outside to potty," Jetrel said.

"No, you can't do that. The doors have alarms on them. I think the girls had some newspapers set down for him in the other room."

Jetrel nodded and took the puppy to the other room. He returned a few minutes later.

"Did he go?" Lydia asked.

"Yeah, he's pretty smart. He seemed to know exactly what I wanted him to do."

"I think we need to come up with a name for him," Lydia said. "Any ideas?"

"I think I'll call him Sam."

"Why Sam?"

"He was a friend of mine," Jetrel said. "The first and only friend I've ever had. Raiel killed him."

"I'm sorry," Lydia said. She walked over to Jetrel and put her arms around him. She wanted to say something to comfort him, but before she could think of anything, the door alarm went off.

"Someone broke in," Lydia said.

Jetrel and Lydia ran into the hall, following the sound of the alarm. As they neared the back door, they saw Father Stephens staggering toward them. Jetrel grabbed the old priest and helped him to the ground. He had been shot several times in the back.

"What happened?" Jetrel asked.

"Raiel," Father Stephens said, "he was following me. I tried to run, but he shot me. I managed to get here, but he won't be far behind me."

"I'm going to call 911," Lydia said.

"No," Father Stephens said. "It's too late for me. I can already see the veil between this world and Heaven beginning to fade."

"No," Jetrel said. "I can't lose you too."

"Please don't feel sad about my death, for I am returning to God's fold. I can already feel the light and peace beckoning me home."

"I don't think I can do this without you," Jetrel said. Tears were running down his face as his emotions began to churn again.

"You can do this, Jetrel," Father Stephens said. "I believe in you. I was wrong earlier when I said that you cannot change. Anyone can redeem themselves, no matter how far down the dark path they've gone. If they're able to fight against the darkness and return to the righteous path, then they can find redemption. It doesn't matter what others think. What matters is that they know they've changed. I've seen how much you've changed, and no matter what happens, I know that you are a good person and that you will do whatever you must to protect the key."

"Thank you, Father," Jetrel said. "I wish I had the same faith in myself that you do."

"You've changed. I've seen it with my own eyes. I know the goodness that lies within your soul, and I will tell everyone in Heaven of your great deeds. Even though others may see you as one of the fallen, you shall forever remain as one of the saints in my eyes."

Jetrel began to sob. He lay his head against Father Stephens' chest as he knelt in the growing pool of blood. Father Stephens reached up, stroked Jetrel's hair with one hand, and took Lydia's hand with the other.

"Quite a touching scene," Raiel said. He was leaning against the doorway, smiling at them.

"Murderer!" Jetrel yelled. He jumped up and tackled the smiling angel, driving him out the door. Lydia started to stand to follow them, but Father Stephens pulled her back down to him.

"Lydia," Father Stephens said. "I have to tell you something quickly before it's too late."

"What is it?" Lydia knelt next to him again, taking his hands in her own. They were very cold.

"You have to help Jetrel. I had another vision in which I saw him fall in the battle against Raiel. Raiel then took the key and opened the gate of the Abyss himself. You can't let this happen. You have to help in whatever way you can to keep Raiel from winning and taking the key for himself."

"I'll do what I can, Father, but what happens if we succeed? Then what do we do with the key?"

"You will have to destroy it," Father Stephens said. His voice was fading slowly as he struggled to speak. "It can only be destroyed by a powerful weapon, like an angel's sword. The only way to truly keep the gate from being opened is to destroy the key. It is better that it be destroyed than to let it fall into Lucifer's hands."

"We will do whatever we can," Lydia said.

"I know you will make me proud," Father Stephens said. He smiled at Lydia a moment before closing his eyes. Lydia felt his hands go limp in hers, so she gently laid them upon his chest before standing up and going after Jetrel.

CHAPTER 44 - MIDDLELAND

Jetrel and Raiel were wrestling on the ground when Lydia reached them. Each was trying to get to the gun that had been knocked from Raiel's hand. In the distance, sirens could be heard approaching the club.

"The police are on their way," Lydia said. "We've gotta get out of here, Jetrel."

Jetrel looked back at Lydia, which gave Raiel an opportunity to knock him away and grab the gun. Raiel stood with the gun pointed at Jetrel.

"Give me the key," Raiel shouted at Lydia.

"We don't have time," Jetrel said. "The police are almost here. Even if you shoot us, you won't be able to escape."

"Then what do you suggest?"

"I suggest we take the battle to Middleland."

"What's Middleland?" Lydia asked.

"Middleland resides between Heaven and Hell," Jetrel said. "It's the field where the battle of the angels took place. When the battle concluded, the ground was saturated with the blood of the angels, so God broke it away from Heaven and placed it as a boundary between Heaven and Hell. No one sets foot there anymore. It is sacred ground upon which none are willing to tread. It is a place of death and sorrow."

"Very well," Raiel said. "The angels fought there once, and it's only fitting that they do so again. We will battle with swords only. No armor, no shields. We will find out which of us is truly the greatest warrior. Which of us will take the key, though?"

"I will," Lydia said.

"If you take the key," Raiel said, "then you must swear to give it to whichever one of us is victorious in the battle."

"I swear," Lydia said. "I'll go get the key."

Lydia ran back into the club, followed by Raiel and Jetrel. She ran into the dressing room and grabbed the key from beneath the towels in the linen closet. When she turned back, Jetrel and Raiel each grabbed one of her shoulders and began to chant. She started to get dizzy and nearly fainted. Once the episode passed, she opened her eyes and looked around.

Lydia found herself alone on an endless expanse of lush grass, taking in her surroundings in a state of awe and shock. The field ran many miles wide and had no defining landmarks of any sort. Flanking it on one side was the vast wasteland of Hell. The terrain reminded her of pictures of Mars she had seen on television. The land was parched red rock, dotted with mountains, spires, and chasms. There were lakes of fire surrounded by geysers of flames, volcanoes, and rivers of lava running across the land. The whole place was dimmed by a sulfurous haze that rose into the air like smoke. Creatures more hideous than anything she could ever imagine crawled and cowered amidst the crags and caverns, all looking skyward at the battle about to take place.

Directly opposite Hell, she saw Heaven and the fear that had begun to creep into her mind dissipated, replaced by a sense of peace and love as she looked across the rolling hills and meadows. She saw all the most beautiful places she had ever seen on Earth, all unspoiled and untouched, despite the presence of the people in them. They were watching the battle above them with fear in their eyes. The fact that those in Heaven were scared made her realize the importance of what was happening.

Directly above her were Raiel and Jetrel, their enormous wings beating delicately at the air around them. They faced each other and circled, neither wanting to make the first move. Raiel's wings were so white, they seemed to glow with a golden sheen that sparkled like sunlight off water. His feet were bare, and he was dressed in a white, flowing shirt and pants that seemed to move with him. His blond hair was short, but still flowed beautifully in the breeze. In his hand, he held a magnificent sword with a polished gold hilt and flawless silver blade. His features were as soft and angelic as one would expect to see, but his mouth was twisted into an evil sneer.

Jetrel's black wings didn't shimmer like Raiel's, but almost seemed to absorb the light around them. Lydia felt that if she were to touch them, she would be pulled into them like a black hole. He was dressed in the same fashion as Raiel, but his clothes were black. His hair was longer than Raiel's and flowed in much the same way. His features were dark and frightening, but in his eyes, Lydia could see the softness that he had so recently developed. He held a sword with a jagged copper hilt and beautiful silver blade.

It was then that she noticed that the clouds had risen above Heaven and Hell, obscuring their landscapes. The clouds formed walls behind each angel, seeming to seal them into this plane. Purple lightning noiselessly streaked across the expanse from the Hell side toward the Heaven side, only to be met in the middle by noiseless golden lightning from Heaven. The air all around Lydia was streaked with lightning, each bolt met by one from the opposite side. The heavy black clouds on the Hell side seemed to be absorbing the light from the air around it, while the soft white clouds on the Heaven side were bursting with bright white light.

Lydia lay back on the soft grass and watched the lightning streak sideways through the sky above her. Then one purple bolt struck Jetrel, while one golden one hit Raiel. Each angel screamed when the lightning struck them, but neither made any move to escape it. Then when the lightning released them, both angels looked stronger. It wasn't a physical change that she could see, but an air of power they exuded. She knew that Jetrel didn't want to draw upon the power that had been given to him by Hell, but he had no choice. He had been healed when he'd entered Middleland, but he'd had to draw on Hell's energy for strength.

It was then that Lydia realized that the throbbing in her ribs was gone. She reached down and felt where her broken ribs had been, but there was no pain. Then she realized that all her recent wounds were gone.

Her attention was quickly drawn back to the scene above her as she heard Raiel shout. He lifted his sword and lunged at Jetrel. Jetrel knocked the blade away and flew back. He brought his blade down toward Raiel, who blocked it with his own. Sparks flew as the two blades connected, and a heavy clang echoed across Middleland. Lydia looked at the clouds obscuring Heaven and Hell and the lightning that continued to streak across the sky. She couldn't see the denizens of either place, but she somehow knew that they could still see the battle raging above them.

Then she heard a slow, steady rumbling in the distance. She thought it was thunder at first, but as it got louder, she realized it was war drums. The drums were then joined by dark, deep chanting. Then Heaven started in with its own chanting prayers. The two conflicting sounds continued to rise, each trying to overpower the other. The melodies mixed into an eerily beautiful song that seemed to be weaving the story as it was playing out. The eerie but beautiful melody made her uneasy and excited at the same time.

CHAPTER 45 - TO BATTLE

Jetrel and Raiel circled each other slowly, neither paying attention to their changing surroundings. Both knew that any lapse in concentration would be fully taken advantage of by the other, so they circled and waited.

It was Raiel who first broke the stalemate. He shouted and lunged at Jetrel, who easily swept the blade aside and winged backward. He brought his own blade up to strike, only to have it blocked by Raiel's. The blades clanged and sparks flew as if protesting the contact. The two angels shoved away from each other and withdrew to regroup. They were both at full strength and the battleground was even. Each looked for an advantage, but could see none.

Jetrel finally broke the uncomfortable stillness by darting at Raiel and swinging at his side. Raiel barely got his blade up in time to catch the blow, and Jetrel used the moment to swing at him with his free hand. His fist caught Raiel across the face, knocking him back and allowing Jetrel to spin and slash him quickly across the hip. Raiel grunted and made a feeble swing of his own, which was easily dodged.

"You're slow," Jetrel said.

Raiel ignored the comment and gave chase. Jetrel saw that he was being pursued, tucked his wings in to his sides, and dove toward the ground. Raiel followed and Jetrel pulled up just before colliding with the ground. Raiel did likewise. Jetrel spun and swung wildly, hoping to catch Raiel off guard. Raiel was watching for the move and swooped beneath the blade, slashing across Jetrel's calves with his own. Jetrel spun to meet Raiel, and their swords collided again; this time, the blades seemed to wail as well as throw sparks.

Raiel and Jetrel both pushed each other, trying to force the other into a mistake. Their blades hummed as they flew through the air, ending in a wail and a shower of sparks as they connected.

Raiel kicked Jetrel, knocking him back and putting some distance between them.

"Are you backing down already?" Jetrel asked.

"Not from you," Raiel said. "I just want to know what Lucifer intended to do with the key if he got it."

"You're stalling."

"Fine, if you don't know the answer, then I'll go ahead and finish you quickly."

"You could never hope to beat me, but I guess there's no harm in filling you in," Jetrel said. "The Key of the Abyss is used to open a gate on Earth to release the plagues of insects that were supposed to torment humanity as the fifth sign of the Apocalypse. Lucifer figured out where it was located and demons were able to find a way into the chamber. With the key of the Abyss, I was supposed to open the gate, which would allow the demons to swarm the Earth. Then humanity would be his."

"That's a pretty bold plan. You should have known that it wouldn't work."

"All I know is that I had a mission," Jetrel said. "The mission may have changed, but I intend to see it through. Lucifer will not get his hands on the key."

Raiel swung his blade, catching Jetrel by surprise. The sword caught him in the abdomen, slicing him from his left hip nearly to his right shoulder. Jetrel fell back, trying to spin out of Raiel's reach as he clutched at the wound. He didn't think the blade had hit any organs, but the wound was still deep. He tried rolling back to face Raiel, but faltered as he felt a sharp pain in his wing. He screamed as he tried to move his wing and felt the flesh tear. Jetrel tried to fly away from Raiel, but he spun toward the ground, his good wing driving the spin. He landed on his shoulder, knocking it out of socket.

Jetrel lay on the ground, his head ringing. He opened his eyes when he felt it would be alright to do so without losing consciousness. Raiel was standing in front of him, his sword lying on his right shoulder. He was smiling. Jetrel felt around with his good arm, trying to find his sword. Raiel lifted the sword from his shoulder and drove the blade through Jetrel's hand, pinning it to the ground. Jetrel screamed.

"It doesn't look like you're in very good shape," Raiel said. "That's going to make it difficult to complete your new mission."

Jetrel looked up at Raiel, as he leaned on his sword looking down at him. Then the smile left his face. The blade of a sword burst from the front of his stomach. The blade slid back through, opening the dam and allowing Raiel's blood to spill onto the ground.

Raiel grabbed his sword and turned. Lydia stood there, holding Jetrel's sword. Her eyes had taken on a frightening darkness.

"What are you doing?" Raiel asked. "You swore that you wouldn't interfere in this fight."

"No," Lydia growled. "I swore to give the key to the winner. I said nothing about influencing the outcome."

Raiel stumbled forward, swinging his blade. He knew he needed to finish this quickly before he was unable to. He lunged at Lydia, but stumbled as Jetrel grabbed his foot causing his swing to go wide. Lydia took advantage of the opportunity and drove Jetrel's blade through Raiel's chest. Raiel stared at her in disbelief as he dropped to his knees. He fell to the side and Lydia let go of the sword.

Lydia stepped back and watched in horror as Raiel struggled to get up several times before dropping limply to the ground. She stared at Raiel's body for several seconds before kneeling next to Jetrel.

"Are you alright?" Lydia asked.

"I've been better, but I'll live. How are you liking your first visit to Middleland?" Jetrel asked. He looked up at Lydia and smiled.

"It's great, but it seems to defy all physics."

"Physics is a human invention," Jetrel said, as he struggled to stand. "They use it to explain the unexplainable. Do you have the key?"

"Yeah," Lydia said. She held it out to show him. "We have to destroy it."

"How do we do that?"

"Father Stephens said that we would need a powerful weapon like the sword of an angel, or something," Lydia said.

"We can use Raiel's sword," Jetrel said, "but you'll have to wield it. It's a holy weapon, so I can't touch it."

"Can't you use your sword?"

"I don't think so. My sword is an evil weapon and not nearly as powerful as an angel's blade. Only the most powerful of the fallen still have their original swords, while the rest of us had our weapons made for us in the depths of Hell. They can kill angels, but aren't as well-crafted as their blades. Now pick up Raiel's sword and hand me the key."

"If I give you the key, won't you be summoned back to Hell?"

"We'll have to do it quickly and hope that we can destroy it before he can summon me back," Jetrel said, as he picked up his sword and sheathed it. Lydia picked up Raiel's sword and was enveloped in a golden glow. Her features softened and her eyes took on a golden hue. She looked like an angel as she held the key out to Jetrel. When Jetrel grabbed the key, his vision began to blur, and the world around him began to spin. Lydia lifted the sword and Jetrel held the key out for her to strike. As Lydia swung the sword, Jetrel's vision went dark.

When his sight returned, he saw that he was in Lucifer's throne room, surrounded by a legion of demons.

CHAPTER 46 - HELL

Jetrel stood in front of Lucifer's throne, all eyes upon him. He looked down at his hands. Both were once again pink with life, instead of red with blood. He held the key tightly in his left hand, knowing full well that he would be expected to turn it over. He stretched his wings and realized that they were healed. He looked at the hundreds of demonic faces surrounding him, watching him with curious interest and violent intentions.

Jetrel then looked at the dark figure seated on the throne in front of him. He looked nearly human, with the exception of the large reptilian wings folded behind him. He was dressed in all black and was leaning forward on his throne. His hands were folded and resting on the pommel of his sword, its tip stabbed into the floor. He rested his chin on top of his hands as he regarded Jetrel.

"I see it's been a productive trip," the man on the throne said.

"It's definitely been an interesting one, Lucifer."

"How dare you call the master by his old name?" one of the demons behind him asked. It bared its teeth and charged at Jetrel.

"Leave him be," Lucifer said. His voiced lifted, nearing a shout. The demon approaching Jetrel flinched as if he'd been struck and quickly darted back into the mass of demons behind him.

"I don't believe Jetrel has been feeling much like himself lately," Lucifer continued. "I believe that we should show him a little bit of courtesy and allow him the chance to explain his actions before we condemn him for them. After all, he must have had a good reason for jeopardizing the mission and attempting to destroy the very item he was sent to Earth to retrieve. I assume he also has a reason for wearing that abomination in my presence."

Lucifer pointed at the cross hanging from Jetrel's neck. Jetrel looked down at it and nearly grabbed it protectively, but stopped himself before it touched his skin and burned him.

"I have nothing to explain," Jetrel said. "I have been in complete control of my actions and if I had it to do over again, I would destroy the key in an instant." Jetrel felt his pulse rising. The feeling of bloodlust began to quicken his mind. He felt the familiar evils returning to his thoughts, swarming like locusts across his brain. He knew that the feelings would get worse the longer he was there, so he needed to find a way to destroy the key quickly before he changed his mind about it.

"I'm trying hard to ignore these blasphemous rants of yours," Lucifer said. "I heard enough of them from you while you were on Earth traipsing around with that whore from the strip club. Now give me the key, return to your duties, and I will forget about everything that you've said and done during your time on Earth."

"I will give you nothing," Jetrel said. The collection of demons surrounding him gasped in unison and began muttering amongst themselves. They were used to crawling through their miserable existences, flinching at any contact with authority. Now the most powerful amongst them was being insulted by someone who was once one of their own. One of the cowering dogs had emerged from the pack to bite the hand of its master, and the rest of the pack knew that retribution would be swift and brutal.

Instead of lashing out, as everyone expected, Lucifer laughed. It was a bitter, painful sound that could drive a man insane. Jetrel tightened his grip on the key and waited for the attack.

"Do you truly think that you can keep the key from me? Perhaps I should show you a little bit of the torment I have in store for you should you continue to defy me." Lucifer smiled, his thin lips pulled back to reveal sharp fangs. He simply waved his arm and the air in front of Jetrel shimmered, forming an image.

The image was of Raiel. He was tied by his arms and legs inside of a shallow stone box. His limbs were stretched painfully to each corner and his wings were missing. Jetrel rubbed at his own arms, seeming to feel the pain along with Raiel. Then the box quickly filled with lava, which ran in through several large holes in the bottom of the box. Raiel screamed, but it was cut short as the lava washed over him. The lava sloshed wildly as Raiel thrashed beneath it, his flesh being melted from his body.

Jetrel fell to his knees. His own flesh felt as if it was being seared from his body. He screamed and clutched at his throat as he felt the lava filling his airways. He fell to the ground, writhing in agony more intense than any he had ever felt. He clutched at the key, making sure it wouldn't be lost in his pain-induced seizures.

Then as quickly as it started the pain subsided. He stood up and looked once more at the image in front of him. All that was left in the stone trough was a red glowing skeleton, still tied at the hands and feet. The bones were quickly covered by muscle as Raiel's body began to regenerate. Soon he would be whole again, and as soon as he was, the lava would wash over him again. It was a vicious cycle that would continue for eternity. Jetrel truly pitied Raiel for the torment he would endure.

Jetrel looked away from the image, fearing that once the torment resumed, he would be immersed in it again. He wiped the sweat from his brow with a shaking hand as he got to his feet. He felt like throwing up and nearly collapsed onto the floor due to his shaking legs.

"Have you seen enough?" Lucifer asked.

"More than enough," Jetrel said.

"Then are you ready to give me the key?"

"No," Jetrel said. "If you want it, then you'll have to take it from me."

Rage flashed across Lucifer's face. His patience had reached its limit. He was used to having everyone cower and beg him for mercy, not talk back to him and disobey his commands. He pulled his sword from the ground and charged at Jetrel.

Jetrel drew his sword as the demons surrounding him scrambled away. Jetrel blocked Lucifer's attack and spun out of the way. Lucifer turned and attacked with a flurry of blows that Jetrel struggled to block. Jetrel couldn't keep this up for long. He was a good swordsman, but Lucifer outmatched him.

Jetrel knocked Lucifer's sword away and jumped aside. He rolled to his feet just as Lucifer attacked again. He blocked the attack, but was being forced backward into a wall. Jetrel tried to block another attack but missed, and Lucifer's sword cut deeply into his arm. Jetrel dropped his sword and screamed. Lucifer delivered a hard kick to the chest, knocking Jetrel onto his back. Lucifer stepped up and swung his sword in a killing arc, which Jetrel blocked with the key of the Abyss.

Lucifer's sword connected with the key, cleaving it in two. The key exploded as the holy energy inside was released, knocking everyone around it back. The explosion was deafening and shrapnel peppered everyone. Golden flames tore through the room, scorching everyone around, Jetrel included. The demons in the room screamed in surprise and agony. When the flames died out, most of the demons lay motionless on the ground.

Jetrel lay on the ground as well. His body was burned, broken, and bleeding. He was wondering what had happened to Lucifer when he heard him scream in rage. Lucifer got up, his flesh blackened and smoking. He grabbed his sword from the floor and ran at Jetrel. Jetrel watched, unable to move, as Lucifer lifted his sword and brought it down upon him.

CHAPTER 47 - AFTERMATH

Lydia woke in an unfamiliar alley with Sam licking her face. She pushed the puppy away and sat up, her head pounding as if she had just woken up after an all-night bender. She stood up slowly, stumbling to the closest wall to stabilize herself. She leaned heavily against the wall and looked around the alley, hoping to see Jetrel, but she didn't. She leaned her back against the brick and slowly slid to the ground. Sam climbed onto her lap and sat looking up at her.

Lydia sat on the ground, absently petting Sam as she stared blankly at the opposite wall. Jetrel hadn't made it back to Earth, which could only mean that he had been taken back to Hell. It was unfair. They had been so close to destroying the key and securing Jetrel's redemption. Even if he had been taken back to Hell, at least he would have succeeded in destroying the key. Instead, he had been taken back to Hell with the key still in his possession. It would be a simple matter for Lucifer to take it from him and use it. Now it was only a matter of time before the gate of the Abyss was opened and the demons swarmed the Earth. Their failure meant the world's destruction.

Lydia lowered her head into her hands and started crying. It wasn't that they'd failed their mission or that the world was going to be destroyed that bothered her the most; it was the fact that she would never get to see Jetrel again, and that hurt her more than anything else could have.

Sam sat up and started licking Lydia's hands. Lydia looked down at Sam before picking him up and hugging him. This was Jetrel's puppy, and it was the only thing she had left of him. She didn't know what else to do, so she sat on the cold concrete, hugging Sam and praying. She concentrated on Jetrel and prayed for his soul, trying desperately to make her feelings known to God. As if knowing what she was doing, Sam sat quietly and allowed himself to be held until Lydia's prayers were finished.

Finally, Lydia opened her eyes and released her grip on Sam, who jumped down and began running around the alley randomly sniffing. Lydia had gotten up and started walking out of the alley when Sam started barking. She turned back to see Jetrel lying on the concrete, hands up as if to defend himself. He opened his eyes and looked around wildly before seeing Lydia standing there.

"I can't believe you're here!" Lydia said. She ran over to Jetrel and hugged him.

"I can't either."

"What happened?" Lydia asked. She got up and helped Jetrel to his feet. "Where's the key?"

"It's destroyed," Jetrel said.

"Thank God!" Lydia said. "Does that mean you've been redeemed?"

"I guess so," Jetrel said. "God must have forgiven me."

"Are you going to be returning to Heaven?"

"I don't know," Jetrel said. He reached back to where his wings should have been. He knew he wouldn't be able to feel them while on Earth, but it was more habit than anything. Even though he couldn't physically feel them, he knew that he would sense them and he sensed nothing. "No, my wings are gone."

"What does that mean?" Lydia asked.

"It means I'm human." Jetrel reached down and grasped the golden cross hanging from his neck. He expected to be burned by it, but instead, the metal felt cool and comforting in his hand.

"So you're not going back to Heaven?"

"Not for a while, anyway," Jetrel said, "and not as an angel."

He looked at Lydia and smiled. He was a human now. He hadn't been made an angel, but when it came down to it, he thought that being human was even better. Now, instead of being submersed in only one type of emotion, he would have the opportunity to experience them all—the good ones as well as the bad.

"How about we get out of here, so you can start enjoying your newfound freedom?" Lydia asked.

"I would love that," Jetrel said, "and I can't think of anyone else I'd rather enjoy it with."

Jetrel bent down and picked up Sam, who started licking his face. Jetrel petted him for a moment before taking Lydia's hand and smiling at her. They turned and left the alley, both of them happy with every aspect of their lives. After all, there were a lot worse things in the world than being human.